P9-DLZ-117

GOODBYE, MR. TERUPT

Also by Rob Buyea

GOODBYE, MR. TERUPT

ROB BUYEA

DELACORTE PRESS

This is a work of fiction. Names, characters, places, and incidents either are the product of the author's imagination or are used fictitiously. Any resemblance to actual persons, living or dead, events, or locales is entirely coincidental.

Text copyright © 2020 by Rob Buyea
Jacket art copyright © 2020 by Chelen Ecija

All rights reserved. Published in the United States by Delacorte Press, an imprint of Random House Children's Books, a division of Penguin Random House LLC, New York.

Delacorte Press is a registered trademark and the colophon is a trademark of Penguin Random House LLC.

Visit us on the Web! rhcbooks.com

Educators and librarians, for a variety of teaching tools, visit us at RHTeachersLibrarians.com

Library of Congress Cataloging-in-Publication Data is available upon request.
ISBN 978-0-525-64798-0 (hc) — ISBN 978-0-525-64799-7 (lib. bdg.) — ISBN 978-0-525-64800-0 (ebook)

The text of this book is set in 12-point Goudy Old Style.

Printed in the United States of America
10 9 8 7 6 5 4 3 2 1
First Edition

Random House Children's Books supports the First Amendment and celebrates the right to read.

Penguin Random House LLC supports copyright. Copyright fuels creativity, encourages diverse voices, promotes free speech, and creates a vibrant culture. Thank you for buying an authorized edition of this book and for complying with copyright laws by not reproducing, scanning, or distributing any part in any form without permission. You are supporting writers and allowing Penguin Random House to publish books for every reader.

For my Mr. Terupt fans, who've been asking
for a fourth book. This one is for you.

summer

Peter

When it came to the gang, we were in the business of making memories. Whether pulling killer pranks or attempting unbelievable stunts—my specialty—or tackling over-the-top projects together, we had a way of doing things that people would talk about for a long time. The kind of stuff that inspired. And this year was no different. This year we needed memories that would last us a lifetime—because after saying goodbye, that's all you have left to hold on to.

I kicked things off for us at the Summer Sound Festival, which was this huge weekend party held outdoors on the Long Island Sound. There were tons of food trucks and vendors, live music and entertainment, and people. It was the place to be. All of our parents went, but we ditched them and met up with each other as soon as we got there.

For all the hype, the festival really wasn't anything that great. The music lineup was just a bunch of local nobodies, and the vendor stuff was even lamer, but Lexie dragged us through tent after tent because no way could she miss out on any shopping.

"Do we really need to walk through all this?" I complained.

"Don't be a sourpuss," Jessica replied. "Look at it this way: maybe you can find some pretty jewelry to buy for Lexie."

"Yeah, that's the attitude," Lexie said, batting her eyelashes at me.

She loved me now, but before long she'd be ready to kill me. That was our relationship—hot and cold.

It was borderline torture, but I tagged along like her lost puppy (her real foo-foo ankle-biter, Margo, was at home because of a strict festival policy—no dogs allowed). I got why Danielle liked the artist booths with the paintings and drawings, and why Anna liked the photography stuff. What killed me was the way Luke was all into the vendors displaying their inventions. He was fascinated by their creativity. Even Jeffrey seemed interested. Maybe not at the booths selling handmade doll clothes or quilts, but he was down with the metal and woodworking stuff. He got excited when he found a small toy wooden train that he was able to buy for his little brother, Asher. I got excited when I found a concession stand in the back of the fourth tent. I was starving, but Lexie wasn't about to stop shopping, so I grabbed a super chili dog for the road. They piled the cheese and onions on top of that thing. The bigger the mess, the tastier the food. I stuffed it in my mouth and chomped down.

"Mmm," I moaned. Mustard spurted out the back end and landed on my shirt.

"Ugh, Peter. Are you serious? I can't take you anywhere," Lexie said, groaning.

"It's just mustard," I said. I swiped the blob off my shirt with my finger and stuck it in her mouth.

Lexie made an awful face and jerked away. "You're disgusting!" she screeched. "I hate you!" She hauled off and punched me in the chest.

"Yeah, but you love me," I teased, and laughed.

Lexie huffed and stomped off, but she didn't really hate me. Consider this a warm-up, because she was nowhere near as mad as she would get. The mustard-finger trick was a good one, but my best idea was yet to come. I stuffed the rest of the dog in my mouth and followed her.

After what felt like an eternity, Lexie finally found something she liked: a toe ring with a sea-glass jewel. It was cool and, surprisingly, it wasn't the most expensive thing there. But she wouldn't let me buy it because she was still playing mad.

"You're being stubborn," I said.

"I don't care," she snapped.

I tried, but whatever. When she finished paying, I took the lead and found the nearest exit. It was a beautiful day, and the last thing I wanted was to spend every minute of it under cover. Enough was enough.

The one cool thing about the festival was all the outdoor games the organizers had put out for people to use. There were volleyball nets, bocce ball sets, and Can Jam courts spread out along the beach. Most everything was being used, but I spotted a free Spikeball kit.

"C'mon, let's try it," I urged.

We kicked our shoes and socks into a pile and ran over to play. Basically, Spikeball is what the name implies. Players stand, surrounding a small circular trampoline-style net, and take turns spiking a rubber ball onto it. If you miss on your turn, the other team scores. There might be some other rules involved, but that's how we did it. We played guys against girls. That might sound unfair, but there were four of them and only three of us, and Luke was definitely the worst, so it was actually pretty even. It was fun, but after a while I had to make it more exciting. I wound up and whaled the ball into the air instead of onto the net.

"Peter!" everyone cried.

The ball sailed into the Sound. Anna was the first to run after it, and then Jeffrey took off, determined to beat her. Next thing I knew, we were all racing across the sand. We had shorts and T-shirts on, but no one was wearing a swimsuit. Didn't matter. I sent Lukester swimming. His arms and legs flailed every which way after I shoved him. Poor kid didn't stand a chance. He belly-flopped into the waves, and the best part was that his crash-landing splashed water all over Lexie too.

"Peter!" she screeched. She kicked and slapped at the

water, trying to get me wet, but she wasn't even close. I laughed at her, but then Jessica soaked me with a sneak attack from the side. It was game on.

We must've looked like we were straight out of one of those ridiculous Disney Channel summer beach movies. The bunch of us goofing around, jumping and splashing and having fun in the water. It was great—until Lexie started screaming. And I mean screaming.

"Lexie, are you okay?" Jessica asked.

She didn't respond. Or couldn't.

"Lexie," Anna tried.

"Lexie," Danielle repeated.

Still nothing.

"Lexie, tell me what's wrong," I demanded, hoping my forceful tone would get her to talk.

But she just continued screaming. When I saw the way she was hobbling out of the water, I figured she had stepped on a sharp shell and had cut her foot, or maybe she'd been bitten by a crab. Both of those things can hurt—not as much as her carrying-on would indicate, but this was Lexie we were talking about. She'd scream if a butterfly landed on her. I was kind of hoping for some blood, because with a little blood in the water we could get lucky and maybe attract a shark, which would've been totally awesome—but she wasn't bleeding. All this drama-queen stuff and no blood. Classic Lexie. I was ready to tell her to suck it up and stop being a baby, but then she plopped down in the sand, clutching her leg. She was crying for real.

"It's a jellyfish sting," Luke said, pointing to the red welt that wrapped around her calf and shin.

"I don't wanna die," Lexie whined.

"You're not going to die," Luke assured her. "Lie back and try to relax."

The girls kneeled by her side, doing whatever they could to comfort her.

"Try not to rub or itch it. That'll only make it worse," Luke told her.

"Ow," she whimpered.

"I didn't see any jellyfish," I said.

"Doesn't matter," Luke replied. "One straggling tentacle is all it takes, but by the looks of her leg, I'd say she got more than that."

"Ow," Lexie continued moaning. "Ow. Make it stop!"

"What can we do?" Anna asked.

"Vinegar," Luke answered. "Vinegar will help ease the sting. I bet one of the food trucks will have some. I'll be right back."

Great, I thought. While Mr. Science Guy goes running off searching for vinegar, poor Lexie has to stay here, suffering.

"Ow," she whined. "It hurts so bad."

"Shhh," the girls whispered. "Close your eyes. Try to relax."

"That's it. Stand back," I ordered. "I can't remember if I read it somewhere or saw it on TV, but peeing on a jellyfish sting is supposed to be the best thing for it. Let me have a go."

"You can't be serious," Jessica replied.

"Try it and you're a dead man," Lexie snarled.

"Just trust me," I assured her.

"Trust *me!*" she exclaimed. "Try it and I'll gouge your eyes out."

"It'll only take a little pee and then you'll be all better," I promised.

"A little pee and you won't live to see tomorrow," she promised, sitting up and glaring at me.

Lexie was seething mad, but you know what, she wasn't whining about her leg anymore. Given the chance, I think whizzing on her would've worked wonders, but the art of distraction did the trick until Lukester came running with a bottle of vinegar. He crouched down and poured it on Lexie's leg and her pain subsided.

I know Luke thinks he was the one who saved the day, but I was the real hero. I didn't slay any dragons, but I was the knight in shining armor who helped his damsel in distress when she was hurting the most. It would've made for an awesome story if I had actually peed on her, but we still had a whole year in front of us. This was only the beginning.

Jessica

Luke rushed over with the vinegar and gently poured it on Lexie's leg. Within minutes her pain eased and she began to calm down. Whether her recovery was psychological or actual, no one could be sure, but we didn't care because all that mattered was Lexie was done dying. "Thanks, Luke," she said, and smiled.

Understandably, Luke was proud. So proud that he felt the need to explain why the vinegar had worked. He wasn't bragging; he was just excited about the science. He was just being Luke.

"A jellyfish sting results in tiny barbs being left in the area of contact," he began. "It's important not to rub or itch the irritation because that can cause the barbs to release more venom and even get lodged into the skin, making it worse. The best approach is vinegar, or if that isn't readily available, you can try dousing the area with ocean water, but not freshwater and definitely not urine, which is a common misconception."

Luke continued explaining, but we were done listening. He should've stopped at the vinegar, because he'd just added insult to injury. Lexie's smile vanished and was replaced by a fierce death stare that she shot at Peter. In fact, she looked ready to kill him. Lexie and Peter had one of those on again–off again relationships, but honestly, I didn't know if they'd ever make it back to on again after this fiasco. I often wondered the same thing about Mom and Dad. Would Mom try again with Dad? Only time would tell—just as it would for Peter and Lexie.

"It's all a matter of osmosis," Luke continued.

"Oh, shut up," Peter growled. "You don't know everything." He kicked sand at Luke and stormed away.

Poor Luke didn't know what to make of Peter's sudden outburst. He was lost. "But I do know," he told us.

"Don't worry about him," Jeffrey said, leaving it at that. There was too much to explain.

I helped Danielle and Anna get Lexie to her feet. We did our best to brush the sand off her back, but that wasn't the main issue: she also had sand in her hair. We made Lexie take her pony out and tip her head down and shake, which turned out to be largely ineffective. She needed a shower, that's all there was to it, but we still assured her she looked fine. It didn't matter that we were stretching the truth because the real problem was in the fact that "fine" would never cut it for Lexie. She was miserable.

"I swear, I'm going to get even with him," she promised us, glaring at Peter in the distance. "And this time I'm not going to play nice."

Honestly, those two were made for each other. I glanced at Danielle and Anna and shrugged. Here we go again, I thought. Danielle better start praying for Peter now.

After Lexie put her hair back in a pony, we went to retrieve our shoes. We found Peter and walked around aimlessly. That jellyfish hadn't only stung Lexie; it had sucked the life out of our party. It seemed like our fun was finished, but then we spotted something that made us smile again—Mr. and Mrs. Terupt, and little baby Hope.

"We wondered if we'd see any of you here," Mrs. Terupt said.

"Are you enjoying the festival?" Mr. Terupt asked.

"Yes! It's been great," Luke exclaimed. "Well, except for—"

"We've had a grand time," I interjected. We didn't need to tell Mr. Terupt everything. Unbeknownst to us, that sentiment went both ways. "Hi, Hope," I whispered, bending lower and peeking inside her stroller. Lexie and Danielle and Anna crowded around to see her too.

"Where are you headed?" Jeffrey asked Mr. Terupt.

"We're taking Hope to see the puppet show they're having on center stage."

"Oh, I forgot about that. My parents mentioned taking Asher to that. It's supposed to be good."

"That's what we've heard," Mrs. Terupt agreed.

"Mr. T, I hate to burst your bubble, but isn't Hope a bit young to appreciate any of that?" Peter asked.

"Babies are sponges, Peter. Hope might not be ready to take in everything, but she'll soak up some of it."

"Mr. T first began reading to Hope when she was still in my belly," Mrs. Terupt said.

Peter went bug-eyes. "Sheesh."

"Hope likes poetry," Mr. Terupt said. "The rhythm, the play on words, the beauty and magic of it."

The language of love, I thought, and smiled. I enjoyed novels in verse, but I was most interested in the poems my father continued sending to my mother. Did poetry also contain healing powers?

"I prefer nonfiction," Luke stated. "Maybe Hope would like to hear something about dinosaurs or snakes?"

"Snakes?" Peter scoffed. "For a baby girl? You definitely don't know everything."

"And neither do you," Lexie jabbed.

"What was the first thing you read to Hope?" Anna asked, wisely continuing the conversation before Peter and Lexie needed boxing gloves.

"A book called *The Penderwicks*," Mr. Terupt answered. "It's the story of four sisters. It reminds Sara of her childhood."

"Mrs. Teach, you have sisters?" Lexie asked. "I didn't know that."

"Yes, you did. We met them at their wedding," I reminded her.

"Oh, yeah."

"I have three," Mrs. Terupt replied. "They all live back home where we grew up."

"You must miss them," I said.

"Yes, I miss them—and their help," she said, "which brings up something Mr. Terupt and I wanted to ask all of you. We're in need of a babysitter, and—"

"I'll do it," the girls jinxed with me. We looked at each other and giggled.

"Looks like you'll need to hold job interviews," Peter teased.

"Or we could do it together," I offered. "We'll be the modern-day Babysitters Club."

"I used to love those books," Mrs. Terupt mused.

"Does that mean guys are excluded?" Luke asked, sounding defeated.

"Of course not," Mr. Terupt replied.

"Yay! Then this is our new project!" Luke cheered.

"Whoa. Time-out," Peter said. "If I'm involved then we need to be called the Babysitters Gang, not any girly club."

"Ugh," Lexie groaned, still angry with him.

"I'm not sure I like the idea of a gang babysitting my daughter," Mrs. Terupt said, "but okay."

"I charge a hundred bucks per diaper change," Peter added.

"You know, I just might pay your fee to see you wrestling with a poopy diaper," Mr. Terupt remarked, keeping a dead-serious face.

Simple as that we became the Babysitters Gang. Our first

day on the job wouldn't be until the end of summer, when Mr. and Mrs. Terupt had beginning-of-the-school-year faculty meetings that they needed to attend, and it would only be for a few hours, during which Hope would probably spend a portion of that time napping, but I was already excited.

Poetry, I thought. I wasn't a poet and I knew it, but perhaps I could try to write a few for Hope. My first would be an ode to her daddy.

Ode to Mr. Terupt
He showed me the way.
Us the way.
Finding himself,
and his missus,
along the way.
And now there's
Hope,
surrounded by love,
and dancing words.
And soon
The Babysitters Gang.

Danielle

Life could be hectic, but Sunday afternoons were reserved for family dinners. No exceptions. It was the one time during the week when Grandma expected everyone to be present at the table—and that included Anna and her mom, Terri, since Terri and my brother, Charlie, were officially engaged. I enjoyed the dinners, the food and the being together, but I was a tad nervous on the Sunday following the festival. I worried the adults might ask Anna and me about our day there, pushing for specifics, and I didn't think the mention of Peter wanting to pee on Lexie would go over well. That wasn't exactly appropriate dinner-table talk. Fortunately, it never came to that because Charlie had news he wanted to share. Unfortunately, things got heated after his big announcement.

"Terri and I have been talking," my brother started, "and we've decided to have our wedding in October, when things on the farm have slowed down. We want to keep it small and we'd like to have the ceremony out back on the ridge. An outdoor wedding has been Terri's dream since she was a little girl."

The ridge Charlie was referring to was on the far side of a field behind the barn. There was a gorgeous view from there. It would be especially beautiful in October when the fall foliage was in bloom. The ridge was one of Charlie's favorite spots on all the farm—mine too—so I thought it was a wonderful idea.

"You mean you want your reception out there," Grandma said, and chuckled. "You've got to get married in the church. That's the only way."

Anna and I grasped hands under the table. That wasn't what Charlie meant.

"It's not the only way, Grandma," my brother tried gently explaining. "People get married outside all the time."

"Yes, but the church is the only *right* way," Grandma countered. There was nothing gentle in her voice.

"But, Grandma—"

"Charlie, you're getting married in the church," Grandma insisted.

"You think if we married someplace other than in the church we wouldn't still be together?" Grandpa retorted. "Hogwash. You could never live without me."

"I've needed the Lord with me every step of the way to

put up with you, so yes, it's a darn good thing we married in His church," Grandma responded.

"I didn't need any church," Grandpa said.

"Well, I did," Grandma snapped. "And so do Charlie and Terri."

Terri's shoulders sagged.

"That's enough," Dad thundered, bringing his fist down on the table and making the dishes jump. "This is Charlie and Terri's wedding, not any of ours. If they want to get married on the ridge, they'll get married on the ridge. The last thing any of us is going to do is ruin their day. Is that clear?"

That was the end of it. It wasn't often that Dad over-ruled Grandma, but his say was final.

Anna squeezed my hand. I was happy for Charlie and Terri, but I wished Grandma wasn't so upset. "You might not always like change, but you can't be scared of it. You need to have faith. Isn't that what you told me, Grandma?" I reminded her.

She huffed. She remembered. She'd told me almost the exact same thing earlier this summer when we began discussing the possibility of me moving away from needles to an insulin pump for my diabetes. My endocrinologist was really in favor of the change because she had seen better control of blood sugars from her other patients using the pump, but I wasn't sure. It wasn't that I didn't want people staring at me because they'd see it. I got used to people staring at me a long time ago. I was just scared. Don't get me wrong, I didn't like needles, but I was comfortable with them. I knew how to use them and I was worried the pump would be too complicated and that I might goof it up. And goofing up your blood sugars could be very serious.

"Danielle, not only are you a smart girl, but you're responsible and independent. Give yourself some credit," Mom had said. "You can do this."

That was when Grandma told me not to be scared of change. "Lord knows there's plenty in this world that I still prefer the old-fashioned way, but I also realize there are instances when change is for the better. Let's not forget, once upon a time women couldn't vote. Imagine that, leaving all of the important decisions to men. If that had never changed we'd all be extinct by now."

Mom and I laughed.

It was after Grandma's pep talk that I made the decision to move to a pump. I didn't have it yet because it had to be ordered and approved by our insurance—which, according to Mom, was a major pain in the butt, excuse her French—but I would be getting one soon. At this point, I was looking forward to it. With time, I hoped Grandma would get used to the idea of an outdoor wedding and maybe even find herself looking forward to it.

It was quiet and uncomfortable around the table after that heated exchange, but that didn't stop Terri from trying to make things better. "Mrs. Roberts," she said to Grandma, "I was hoping you'd go to church with Charlie and me on the morning of our wedding and say a prayer for us, asking the Lord to give us his blessing. There's no one I'd rather have do that for us than you."

Grandma stared across the table at Charlie and Terri. "I'd like that," she said.

Anna and I squeezed hands again. It was going to be okay. Better than okay. Beautiful. And it would've been if I was as responsible as Mom believed.

Later that night I checked my sugars and said a prayer before climbing into bed.

Dear God,

Please comfort Grandma and please be there for Charlie and Terri even though they aren't getting married in your church. They'll be getting married instead on the beautiful ridge you've provided us. Amen.

I should've prayed for myself, but selfish wasn't my style. Not being selfish almost cost me.

anna

I kept it inside, buried deep. I didn't like the way I was feeling and I didn,t want anyone to know—not even Danielle. And not Mom. She was the problem. Well, she and Charlie were.

Lexie and her mom had Vincent, her mom's boyfriend, living with them now, and it didn't mess anything up. Lexie loved Vincent and said everything was better with him around. Charlie hadn't even moved in with us yet and he was already messing things up.

Mom and I used to go out to lunch on weekends. She used to join me in the kitchen while I was plopped down doing my homework. We'd chat about school and she'd make us hot chocolate or some other fun drink. We used to have mother-daughter movie nights, when we'd cuddle on the couch with a big bowl of popcorn. We used to . . . but not anymore. I was happy for Mom, but I didn't want to lose her. I liked Charlie—a lot. But I knew what I was feeling, and like it or not, I couldn't help it. I hoped everything would get better and these dumb feelings would go away after they got married. But it wasn't Mom or Charlie or me and my feelings that I should've been worried about at the wedding.

Jeffrey

Peter needed to get away, so it was a good thing we had wrestling camp. After the stunt he almost pulled at the festival, I was surprised Lexie didn't have Wanted Dead or Alive posters of him hanging around town. I was excited for camp because I had high goals this season. I was on a mission to pin all of my opponents and finish the year undefeated.

We decided to attend the camp at Cornell University. Cornell has one of the best college wrestling programs in the country, so there was going to be a bunch of great coaches and wrestlers there. It was Terupt's idea for us to go, but it was Dad and Asher who gave us a ride to camp and got us registered. Terupt was busy repainting his house and being a dad.

Just like at last summer's camp, we were in a dorm with all

sorts of older high schoolers. What was different was Peter. Must've been he'd learned his lesson last time because he stayed away from the older guys. He didn't get involved in their pranks and shenanigans, so we weren't running around with targets on our backs. This time around, Peter got himself into trouble by complete accident.

It all started on our third day, when we were at our evening session. We had this guy Rex, who was one of the wrestlers on the Cornell team, leading our practice. Rex was jacked. Muscles rippled over his entire body. But it was the tattoo of a bear wearing a red Cornell wrestling singlet drawn on his calf that Peter thought was so cool.

"Nice tat," Peter told him when he came walking by to check on us to see if we were getting the hang of the technique he'd just demonstrated.

"Thanks," Rex said.

"Are you guys the bears?" Peter asked.

"We're the Big Red, but the bear is our mascot."

"Cool," Peter replied. "I'm thinking about getting a lion."

"You are?" I said, surprised. That was the first I'd heard him mention wanting a tattoo. "When?"

"When I turn sixteen, if my mom will let me. I want a lion like the Penn State mascot. That one is awesome."

"Are you guys trying to be wiseasses?" Rex asked, snarling.

I could see Peter was just as confused as I was. "No," he croaked.

"You think you're funny? You little punks," Rex spat. He stared us down for a good ten seconds and then marched off.

Peter turned to me. "What did I say?"

"I don't know, but you sure pissed him off. And somehow, I'm involved again. Way to go."

We spent the rest of that practice staying as far away from Rex as possible. Being a coach, he had the power and authority to torture us anytime and anywhere he pleased—and he had reason to want to punish us. This was even worse than last year's trouble.

When we got back to our room that night I hopped on my laptop and did some research. Turns out Rex had taken third in the country this past season. His lone defeat came at the hands of a guy from—you guessed it—Penn State. Peter and I had had no idea, but Rex thought we were busting his chops about getting beat. It was pretty clear Rex still wasn't over that loss. Nothing about it was funny. He was angry. Real angry.

Fortunately, Rex was cool and chose to ignore us after that and we continued to leave him alone too. We weren't worth his time and we were A-OK with that. So things were still good at camp until our final evening session of the week. The Cornell wrestlers, Rex included, had led that workout and they decided to teach us how to play one of their favorite games to conclude practice. I'd never heard of the game Slap Back. Neither had Peter, but he still proved to be the best.

Basically, Slap Back was a game of tag. To play, we had to take our shirts off and lie on our bellies side-by-side with our partners. Picture pairs of wrestlers spread out all over the wrestling mats. Two kids were picked to stand up and start the game. One was designated the tagger and the other was running for his life to avoid getting tagged. Why? Because you tagged the runner by slapping him on his back—his bare back—as hard as you could. A good smack left a nasty hand-print and almost instantly turned bright red. The best slaps resulted in grotesque welts.

The runner's job was to scurry around the mats until he decided to slide down next to any one of the pairs lying on their bellies. If the runner slid in on the left of the pair, then the guy on the right side became the new runner and had to jump up and take off. Everyone wanted to see someone get smacked, so a lot of times the runner would let the tagger get close before sliding down. The new runner wouldn't have a chance to get away. He was a sitting duck. He'd get whaled and everyone would cheer.

The one blessing was, after getting tagged the roles re-versed, and the guy with the now-red back got a chance to get revenge. Slap Back was a game of painful fun. You loved it until you felt it. But the game went from fun to borderline scary when the counselors decided to join. The last thing you wanted to do was wallop one of them because then you were dead meat.

Sure enough, the inevitable happened. Rex got his turn as tagger. He chased down a squealing camper, look-ing to deliver a fatal blow, but before he got his chance the squealer slid down next to me, which meant Peter was now the runner. Peter scrambled to get out of the way, but there was no escape. Rex hovered, his sights locked on the camper who was number one on his hit list. He delivered a blow on Peter's back that echoed throughout the gym, sending the campers into a wild hysteria, screaming and cheering. To his credit, Peter didn't die. He rose from the ground and tore after the big man, but the damage was done.

At the end of the game the Cornell guys had the campers who got smacked line up like you would for a bodybuilding contest, so that the rest of us could judge their backs. The guy with the reddest, nastiest, most painful-looking back was declared the winner—and that was Peter.

Rex was cool and came up to us after all the fun to check on Peter. "You okay, Penn State?" he asked.

"I wasn't being a wiseass," Peter said. "I didn't know the guy you lost to was from there."

"Yeah," Rex acknowledged.

"I hope you beat him this year," Peter said.

"Thanks. I'm gonna try."

Peter and Rex fist bumped and then Rex left with his buddies.

In the end, it was another successful and memorable camp experience. I learned some new techniques and felt like I got better. I was ready for a killer season.

Peter had a good camp too, but man, did he ever get it bad during Slap Back. Almost hard to believe Lexie could manage to get him even worse, but she was ready when she got her chance.

LUKE

I was in a much better position entering eighth grade than I had been before the start of seventh. For one thing, I knew the layout of the school and where my classrooms were located. And for another, I already knew what classes I was taking. I'd done exceptionally well in seventh grade and had been placed in all of the accelerated courses. This was a significant achievement because accelerated sections in eighth grade didn't simply mean advanced this or advanced that. It meant I was on the accelerated track, taking my first high-school credits—specifically, geometry and biology.

That was precisely why I was so excited about the Babysitters Gang. Not only was it a great project for us, it was the perfect preparation for biology—the study of life. Taking care of baby Hope was true hands-on science. On top of that, it was also a situation where proofs could be applied, and proofs were a big topic in geometry. I was looking forward to proofs because I liked proving things. Proofs relied on truths and theorems and often incorporated if-then statements. The other cool thing about proofs was that they didn't only apply to geometry, but you could use them in science—and in life, too. For example:

IF Peter tries to do anything stupid to Lexie,
THEN Lexie will be determined to get even.

IF the gang gets together for babysitting,
THEN that will be the perfect opportunity for Lexie
to enact revenge.

We arrived at Mr. and Mrs. Terupt's house early in the morning. They were on their way to district faculty meetings, in preparation for the start of school next week. Mrs. Terupt went over everything we needed to know. She showed the girls where to find Hope's supplies: diapers, wipes, bottles, milk, blankets, clothes, toys, books, etc. Peter, Jeffrey, and I stayed back out of the way because that was the part of the project we weren't really interested in, but Mrs. Terupt made sure we were paying attention when she covered the strict guidelines and rules for performing a diaper change and prepping a bottle. NEVER leave a baby unattended when she's on top of the changing table or any other elevated structure, and NEVER heat a bottle in the microwave. I could tell she was feeling uneasy about leaving her daughter, so I tried reassuring her.

"Don't worry, Mrs. Terupt. We've got it under control," I promised her. "We love projects."

She made a funny face. Maybe referring to Hope as a project wasn't the best idea.

"Luke's right," Jessica said, coming to my rescue. "What he means is, you've got all of us here working together to keep Hope happy and safe. So don't worry."

Mrs. Terupt flashed a small smile. Jessica was better with words.

Mr. Terupt gave us his phone number in case we needed anything and then he gently guided his wife out the door. They were going to be late if they didn't get going. We watched them drive away and then we did nothing. Hope was still napping, so there wasn't anything for us to do. I'd been so excited and this project was boring. Peter agreed.

"I'm bored," he complained.

IF Peter gets bored,
THEN he will try to get creative to pass the time.

IF Peter gets creative,
THEN that can spell trouble.

The girls headed upstairs to the family room to watch TV. They took the baby monitor with them so they could hear Hope if she woke up. Meanwhile, I hung in the kitchen with Peter and Jeffrey. Mrs. Terupt had baked cookies for us and we were already getting started on them.

"Hey, what's this thing?" Peter said, noticing a soft black case that was on the floor near one of the kitchen chairs.

"It looks like my mom's scrapbooking case," I said. "Maybe Mrs. Terupt is a scrapbooker? She could be making a baby book for Hope or something like that."

Peter unzipped the top and pulled out a weird-looking funnel that was attached to a length of clear tubing, the sort of hose you'd find on an aquarium filter. "Not sure this is for scrapbooking," he said.

"No," I agreed. I'd never seen such a contraption, and it was obvious Peter and Jeffrey hadn't either.

Peter held the cone over his ear like he was playing telephone. Next he stuck it on his forehead and pretended it was erasing his brainpower—the little he had. Then he put it over his mouth and talked into it, making funny noises. That was when silly turned into exciting.

Jeffrey spotted a switch inside the black case and flipped it. All of a sudden the thing started making noises and the funnel Peter held over his mouth turned into a vacuum. It grabbed onto his lips and sucked them inside. Peter squealed and yanked the sucker off his face. "What the heck!" he yelled.

Jeffrey and I couldn't stop laughing. And after he got done freaking out, bonehead Peter found it funny too. So what did he do? The goofball took the cone and stuck it on his mouth again and made all these crazy fish faces and noises while the cup suctioned his face. Jeffrey egged him on, encouraging him to stick it on his forehead. Of course Peter did. And when he got bored of that, he grabbed me in a headlock and stuck the cone on my cheek. I kicked and squirmed and weaseled my way free, but not before I had a dark red circle on my face to match the red rings Peter wore around his mouth and on his forehead.

"Better give me that before you two break it," Jeffrey said, turning the machine off and taking the funnel and hose from us.

"What in the world do you think that thing is?" Peter asked.

"Not a clue," Jeffrey replied. "Do you know, Lukester?"

"Nope."

"Well, whatever it is, it made me thirsty," Peter said. "I need something to wash down Mrs. T's cookies." He got up, walked to the refrigerator, and peered inside. "Think Mr. T will miss this smoothie if I drink it?" he asked, but he didn't give us a chance to respond. "You know what, I'm drinking it. I'll count it as my payment."

Peter came back to the table and sat down with his vanilla shake. Then he tipped his head back and gulped down half of it.

"Dang, that's sour," he said, grimacing. "Think it's expired?"

"I don't know, but your milk mustache looks stylish with those red lips," I teased.

Peter sneered. Then he slugged down the rest of the sour

shake and slammed the container on the table, doing his best tough-guy act. "Careful, Lukester," he warned. "You don't want me to attack you with the sucker again. Next time I'll use it to pull out your eyeball."

"Shhh—what was that?" Jeffrey said.

We listened. There it was. The first noises coming from Hope's room. The girls came running downstairs into the kitchen—and that was when Lexie proved my proof. Revenge!

Alexia

Teach was cool and let me bring Margo when it was time for the Babysitters Gang. Maybe Hope liked poetry, but she was going to like Margo even more. Mrs. Teach was cool with it too. She was more concerned about going over everything we needed to know before she had to leave. She gave the girls and me the rundown on where to find all the supplies when it was time for diaper changes and feeding Hope. Peter should've paid attention, but he never did. His mistake was my blessing.

After the Teaches left, the girls and I hung out upstairs in the family room, playing with Margo and watching reruns of *Friends*. The guys stayed down in the kitchen. They were busy stuffing their faces with Mrs. Teach's cookies. But you can't eat your cookies without milk.

We were halfway into our second episode when we heard the first noises coming from the baby monitor. Jessica muted the TV and I didn't even have a freak-out. We froze and listened, and there it was again—Hope was awake. We jumped and hurried downstairs, and what should appear to my wandering eyes but Peter, with a thick milk mustache and an empty container in front of him.

"Peter!" I screeched.

"What?"

"What are you drinking?"

"Mr. T had a smoothie in the fridge."

"No, you didn't," I said.

"I did," he replied.

"No, you didn't," I repeated.

"Didn't what?" he snapped, getting short with me. He turned to Jeffrey and Luke, but, like, they just shrugged. They were clueless—all three of them.

"Ohmigod!" I cried. The girls and I lost it. We were dying. This was unbelievable.

"What's going on?" Peter yelled.

"Peter, that wasn't a smoothie," Anna managed to say in between laughs.

"What do you mean?"

"It was Mrs. Terupt's breast milk," Jessica explained, wiping tears from her eyes.

"You idiot!" I squealed.

Peter didn't believe us. "Yeah, right. Whatever," he scoffed. "How does she get her boob juice into a bottle?"

"With that," Danielle said, pointing to the soft black case sitting near the kitchen table. If anyone knew about milking, it was her.

Peter's mouth fell open. He reached up and rubbed the red circle on his forehead.

"You're such an idiot!" I exclaimed.

The look on Peter's face was priceless. I couldn't stop laughing. Even Jeffrey and Luke started cracking up.

"Wait until Teach finds out you drank his wife's breast milk!" I teased.

"No!" Peter cried. "You can't tell him. Please. No," he pleaded.

His whimpering was music to my ears. I had him right where I wanted him. It was time for some fun. "Get down on your knees and beg," I said.

He didn't even hesitate. The boy was desperate. Putty in my fingertips.

"Kiss my feet," I ordered next.

"You're pushing it," he growled.

"I'll tell," I promised.

He puckered up and planted his lips on my toes. Oh, the power I had over him. I would've kept going, had him bark like a dog and roll over, if it weren't for Hope's cries growing louder.

"That's good for now," I said, satisfied. "We need to take care of Hope, but don't worry, I'll let you know when you can wait on me next—and you will, or else your secret won't be secret anymore, Mr. Boob-Juice Drinker."

Peter slunk against the wall and I skipped off to help the girls with Hope. We got the little princess changed and swaddled, and then we fixed her a bottle using Mrs. Teach's extra breast milk from the freezer. Once we had everything, we went back upstairs to the family room where the guys were chilling now too. Peter and Jeffrey were playing with Margo and Luke had the remote.

Anna sat on the sofa and we propped some pillows around her to help her hold Hope. We were doing great, but then, like, Hope got fussy and wouldn't take the bottle. Jeffrey helped us reposition her and showed us what to try with the bottle and then Hope started sucking away. We giggled. She was so cute.

"Guess I learned a few tricks with Asher," Jeffrey said and shrugged.

"Guess so," I said. "Apparently, not all boys are as dumb as Peter."

"Ha ha," Peter groaned.

"What're you watching?" Jessica asked Luke.

"CNN. Catching up on the news," he said.

That was the last thing I wanted to watch and I was about to say so, but then, like, something came on that changed everything. It was a commercial for this home kit called GeneLink that you could use to test your DNA to see if you had the genes that put you at risk for certain diseases. I didn't even know that was a possibility. I mean, I could use that kit and find out if I had the gene for breast cancer, like Mom had. *But then what?*

The commercial ended and Luke changed the station to PBS for Hope, but I couldn't stop thinking about what I'd just seen. I scooped Margo into my arms and hugged her tight.

But then what?

Jessica

Ode to Hope
The Babysitters Gang took care of you
without incident,
except for Peter
stealing your milk.
Shhh!
That's our secret.

"How'd everything go?" your anxious mom asked
the moment she returned.
"Fine," a devilish Lexie replied.
"Only one small mishap with your milk.
But like, we found more in the freezer.
So no biggie."

"A small mishap, huh?" your ever-wise know-better
    father replied,
eyeing Peter.
Jeffrey snickered. "That's right."
"This was the best project ever!" Luke exclaimed.
(No offense, but he refers to you as a project.)
"I learned so much," he carried on.
"I can't wait to do it again."

That sentiment
was shared by all.
We couldn't wait to spend
more time
with you.
And we didn't even know
time
was short.

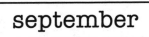

september

Peter

One thing sucked about eighth grade right from the start. The school had made some changes over the summer and T was stuck teaching seventh-grade science, so none of us had him. I didn't think I'd ever be happy about that, but I didn't know what was coming, either.

We tried visiting T after our first day of school, but he was already on his way out when we got to his room.

"Hey, gang," he said.

"You're sure getting out of here in a hurry," I replied.

"No choice. I need to get Hope from daycare. If I'm late we pay more."

"I heard that stuff is expensive."

"Very," he admitted, "so we try to minimize Hope's time there. Sara takes her in the morning since Snow Hill's school day starts later than ours, and I pick her up because I get done earlier."

"So that means you'll be rushing out every day," Luke said, putting two and two together.

"That's exactly what it means, genius," I replied, annoyed.

"For now," T admitted, "at least until wrestling starts. But don't worry. We'll figure something out."

What? I thought.

Bummed, we turned around and left. Everyone headed to the lobby to catch their rides, but I'd forgotten my hat in my locker, so I marched back upstairs.

The weather at the beginning of September had been so hot and sticky that the copy machine on the second floor kept jamming. The teachers got smart and moved the machine from their work room into the hall, where it was less humid, and the dumb thing cooperated. Their mistake was leaving it out, unsupervised, after school.

What do you do when you see an unguarded copy machine in the school hallway? Answer: If you're me, you have fun with it. I dropped my backpack to the side. There wasn't a soul around. I lifted the top and stuck my mouth and face on the glass and pushed the green button. The light inside a copier is way brighter than I realized. It about blinded me, but that just made the photocopy even funnier. I was gonna do another one but then I heard footsteps coming, so I grabbed my bag and booked it out of there. The last thing I needed was some teacher seeing me messing with their machine. Next thing you knew I'd be getting blamed for it not working. Turns out I got blamed for something anyway. When you have my kind of rap sheet, that stuff happens. Good thing I knew how to handle Mr. Lee.

Mrs. Francine, our school secretary, buzzed my classroom the next day, requesting I report to the office. I was stoked to be getting out of math, but I knew something was up.

"Mr. Jacobs, why am I not surprised to see you've landed in my office on only the second day of school?" Mr. Lee began.

"Is that a rhetorical question, sir?" I asked, already pushing his buttons.

"Yes, it's rhetorical!" he hollered. "I'm not surprised because you're the biggest jokester this side of the Mississippi."

"Thank you, sir," I responded, pushing more.

"That wasn't a compliment," he growled.

Mr. Lee was turning redder by the second. I'd never seen that vein in his forehead before, the one that was bulging. He was ready to explode. What had him so angry?

"Mr. Jacobs, do you know what showed up in every single teacher's mailbox this morning?"

"No," I answered truthfully. I had no idea.

"Really?"

I shrugged and shook my head.

"This," he said, holding up a piece of paper.

I had to do a double take. Was that what I thought it was? It was! Someone had photocopied their naked butt!

"That showed up in every teacher's mailbox?!" I exclaimed.

"Yes," Mr. Lee replied.

I burst into laughter. "Awesome!"

"I'm glad you find this so funny, Mr. Jacobs, because it's going to be me getting the last laugh when I take you down for this stunt."

"Me? I didn't do that!"

"Denying it? Well, for your information, you were spotted leaving the second-floor hallway after school yesterday."

"I forgot my hat in my locker and went back for it. That's why I was up there."

"A likely alibi."

"Mr. Lee, that isn't my butt," I argued.

"Prove it."

He asked for it. I wasn't getting blamed for something I didn't do. I jumped from my chair and dropped my shorts, giving Mr. Lee a full moon right there in his office.

"Mr. Jacobs, put that away!" he shouted.

"Look!" I ordered, pointing at my right cheek. "See that scar? It's been there since I was little."

Knock knock.

"Mr. Lee, here is the file you reque—"

"Do not come in here!" Principal Lee ordered. He tried, but it was too late.

Mrs. Francine waltzed in. "Ahh!" she screamed. She dropped the file and ran off, still screaming.

Mr. Lee sighed. "Mr. Jacobs, pull your shorts up."

"Not until you agree there's no way that photocopy is mine."

"I see. I see. Now pull your pants up. We're lucky Mrs. Francine didn't have a heart attack, for God's sake."

I could've been wrong, but I swore I heard a chuckle in his voice when he added that last part. "Mr. Lee, I didn't do it," I said after I was dressed again. "Part of me wishes I could take credit because I think it's super funny. But it wasn't me."

"Mr. Jacobs, we're done here. You can leave now."

"But you haven't even apologized for blaming me for something I didn't do."

"Get out!" he roared.

I bolted. I knew when enough was enough.

"Have a nice day, Mrs. Francine," I sang as I strolled past her desk.

She shrank behind her computer screen and I laughed. I felt pretty cocky strutting my way out the door, but once I was in the hall something came to me I hadn't thought about earlier. I hoped that naked butt sat on the glass *after* I had plastered my mouth on it, and not before.

LUKE

Just when I thought I had my accelerated schedule in order, the school administration decided to insert a one-hour block every other Friday for a period called "advising." The extra minutes were freed up by reducing the length of our classes on these days. Thankfully, this new ordeal was only a biweekly thing, and the entire junior high would be engaged in it, so it wasn't like I'd be missing anything. Still, I wasn't thrilled, because I wasn't convinced it'd be worth it—that is, until I learned who I had for my adviser.

**IF Mr. Terupt says we'll figure something out,
THEN something will happen so the gang
can get together.**

The complete Babysitters Gang made up our advising group. It didn't get any better than that. Did Mr. Terupt have to pull strings to make that happen? I didn't know and I wasn't asking. But suddenly, advising became the part of school I was most excited about.

The goal and description of this new activity was still unclear, but after doing some research on the topic, I learned that advising at other schools and universities focused on the social and emotional growth of students, and it provided guidance and counseling on academic decisions. There was no one I'd rather have had mentoring me on those matters than Mr. Terupt. And I know I speak for the rest of the gang when I say that. Advising was a serious time, but serious was not how Mr. Terupt started our first session together.

"Okay, gang. The number one item Principal Lee has asked us to address with our advising groups today is the now-infamous butt prank."

"The what?" I stammered.

"Peter's latest prank," Lexie answered.

"That wasn't me!" Peter protested.

"Nobody else would even think to do that," Lexie argued.

"Oh, yeah? I think it was you," Peter countered.

"Me!" Lexie screeched. "There's like, no way I would put my tush on a copy machine. I can't even get myself to sit on a public toilet seat. That's like, totes gross."

"What? Do you squat?" Peter asked.

"Yes, I squat. You got a problem with that?" She raised her fist.

"What are you guys even talking about?" I interrupted, looking for clarification.

"Honestly, do you live under a rock?" Lexie said. "The whole school has been talking about the butt prank for two days."

I shrugged.

"Luke, did you happen to notice the photocopy machine in the upstairs hallway on our first day of school?" Jessica asked.

"Sure," I said. "A scientist is always making observations."

"Well, somebody with a creative mind also saw it and came up with the brilliant idea of photocopying his naked butt," she explained.

"Over a hundred copies," Jeffrey added, "that were then stuck in every teacher's mailbox."

My eyes got wide.

"Is that true?" Danielle asked.

"Yup," Peter confirmed. "But how do you know it was *his* butt and not *her* butt? You're jumping to conclusions."

"Peter's right," I said. "The only way we can be certain is to find a hair or some other piece of evidence from the machine and run a DNA analysis."

"A butt hair!" Peter cried. "That's awesome. Hey, Lexie, want to see if you can find one for us?"

"Shut up!" she shrieked. "You're disgusting!"

Peter laughed. "Face it. We'll never know who did it. What's Lee supposed to do, have a butt lineup to identify the criminal?"

"Ugh," the girls groaned.

It *was* an idea.

"I'm going to miss this," Mr. Terupt mused.

Instantly, the banter stopped. Did we hear him right?

"What do you mean? Where are you going?" Peter asked.

"Not me. You," he said. "You're all moving on to high school after this year."

True, but was that what he meant or was he covering for a slip-up? Was he sick? The sudden dread in my stomach wasn't based on science. It was intuition. And it was strong.

"Well, now that we've thoroughly discussed the butt prank, I think we can move on to the next item on my agenda. It's time for a project," Mr. Terupt announced.

Those were the magic words. My worries vanished just as fast as they'd arrived.

"What kind of project?" I asked.

"I was thinking we should put together a time capsule to commemorate our years together."

"Mr. Terupt, please stop talking like this is the end. It's scaring me," Anna said.

"Me too," Danielle agreed.

"It's only the end of junior high school, but since I won't be following you to ninth grade, I thought it seemed like a good idea. But we don't need to do it if you don't want to."

"No, let's do it," Jessica urged. "Each of us should come up with something to contribute. It'll be fun to open it at the end of the year."

"What do we contribute?" I asked.

"Anything," she said. "Anything that will help us reminisce about the good times we've had."

"Oh, boy," Peter said, rubbing his hands together. "So many ideas." He laughed, and Lexie groaned.

"Keep it clean," Mr. Terupt warned.

But "oh, boy" was right. I knew by the end of that first session that advising was going to be great—but I never dreamed it would be the year of projects that it turned out to be.

Jessica

Poetry is . . .
Rhyming.
Poetry is rap.
Poetry is Dr. Seuss and Shel Silverstein—Hope's
    favorites.
Poetry is Kwame Alexander and Elizabeth
    Acevedo—my favorites.

Poetry is Peter
and Lexie
back
and forth
words at rapid fire
comeback

after comeback
they dance.

Poetry is time capsules
commemorating moments,
capturing moments,
and celebrating moments
after times together come to an end.
Poetry is a language of love
arriving in a small, rose-colored envelope,
words from my father
to my mother
about moving
here
to be near us.

Words
sending my thoughts swirling
and breaths catching,
because sometimes
poetry is broken promises,
broken hearts.

Jeffrey

Maybe we didn't have him as our teacher, but Terupt still found Peter and me in between classes and pulled us aside in the hall.

"Hey, guys. I just got an email from Mr. Jennings, the varsity wrestling coach. They're starting open mats soon and I think you should go."

"What're open mats?" Peter asked.

"The high school coaches aren't allowed to practice with their teams in the off-season, but they still have their guys getting together for workouts."

"So it's like a practice without coaches?" Peter asked.

Terupt shrugged. "Sort of. You kinda go and do your own thing. But I'll be there. No rules prohibiting me from attending."

I was all in. "Let's do it," I said. "Just tell me when."

* * *

"When" came two weeks later. Dad gave Peter and me a ride to the high school that night and hung out to watch. Open mats only lasted an hour, but man, did a lot happen in that short time.

We scooted into the locker room to change and the first guy I saw was Zack. I barely recognized him. Talk about a growth spurt.

"Zack Attack," Coach Terupt said, greeting him. "You got big, huh?"

"Yeah, I've grown four inches and jumped up five weight classes since last season. I've been trying to hit the weights because I need to get stronger. I'm not wrestling little twerps like this anymore," he said, gesturing at Peter and me.

"Watch it," Peter warned. "I'll still take you."

Zack smirked. "See you guys out there."

Peter and I changed our shoes and hurried out to the mats and started jogging to warm up. Coach Terupt loosened up with us and then paired off with Zack. Peter and I didn't really know what we were supposed to do so we just copied what they did. After a while, a different high schooler who I didn't recognize came over and asked if we wanted to scrimmage.

"Go ahead," Peter said.

So I did. And I got my butt kicked. I'd never been beaten like that. The kid wiped the mat with me, but I kept fighting. I didn't notice Terupt watching us until we scrambled off the edge of the mat and had to stop.

"Let me show you guys something," Terupt said. "What's your name?" he asked my opponent.

"Freddy."

Terupt showed us this nifty turn from the top position that involved using your legs. Freddy was good with his legs. He'd been crushing me with them all night, but he didn't pay much attention to Coach Terupt.

"Cool," Freddy said after Terupt was done demonstrating. "I've got to use the bathroom."

Terupt shook his head as he watched Freddy walk away. Then he turned to Peter and me. "If you want to be good, you have to be coachable."

Peter and I spent the next ten minutes going over Coach Terupt's move. The more I tried it, the more comfortable I got doing it. It was all about turning the guy's hip so that you could attack his upper body while he's under you, exposing his shoulders to the mat and getting points.

"How'd you like working with Freddy?" Zack asked me after practice.

"He killed me," I confessed.

"Yeah, he's tough," Zack admitted. "But he cuts too much weight."

"What do you mean?"

"Freddy's our one twenty, but I bet he weighs around one thirty-five right now. So don't sweat it if he beat you up. He's got some pounds on you." He grabbed his bag. "See you next time."

"Later."

Peter was ready to go but I'd left my stuff in the locker

room, so I ran to get it. I was surprised when I found Freddy still hanging out in there.

"Hey, what's up," I said.

"You're pretty tough for an eighth grader," Freddy said, giving me some unexpected props.

"Thanks."

"You could be our varsity one thirteen if you wanted," he said.

"You think so?"

"Yeah. You're way tougher than the kid we've got there now. What do you weigh?"

"One twenty-one."

"You could definitely make it," Freddy said. "I cut way more than that to get down to one twenty last season, and I'm gonna do it again. You should go for it. We could be teammates."

"That would be awesome."

"I've gotta split," he said, getting to his feet. "Peace out."

"See you."

Freddy left and I sat there thinking about everything that had just happened. One twenty was my weight class, but there was no way I was beating Freddy. He'd just kicked the crap out of me for fifteen minutes. I was a lean 121, with barely any body fat, but if Freddy could lose the weight, what was stopping me? If I wanted it bad enough, I could make the sacrifice. And I wanted it. Varsity, I thought. That was my new mission.

"Dude, you coming?" Peter shouted after coming into

the locker room to find me. "We've been waiting for ten minutes. You're worse than a woman."

"You haven't been waiting that long, and yeah, I'm coming."

"What're you doing in here?"

"Nothing," I said. "Let's go."

I'd miss being teammates with Peter. It was too bad we couldn't make the move together, but he was a 113-pounder. Sometimes you had to beat your best friend and go it alone.

anna

After all the hoping and wishing I'd done to see Mom and Charlie get engaged, now I just wanted the whole ordeal over so maybe Mom would have some time for *us* again. The only reason I was the tiniest bit excited about the wedding was because it was going to be an incredible opportunity for me to take pictures and show off my photography skills. I wish I could say my feelings changed as their big day drew near, but I'd be lying. It only got worse. The wedding just gave Mom and Charlie more reason to always be together—and less time for her to be with me.

It was going to be a small wedding, but small weddings still required planning. There were flowers to pick out and invitations and music and food and . . . and . . . and. Plus, with the ceremony being held outside on the ridge, there were all sorts of extra details and precautions to consider, like how to get people out there and where they'd sit—and Mom's worst nightmare, what to do if it rained. Even with all that planning, we still didn't think of everything. Needless to say, Mom was preoccupied. But Jeffrey had time for me.

"Danielle, do you think it would it be okay if I brought Asher over to your farm so he could see the cows?" Jeffrey asked when we were at lunch.

"Sure," she replied. "I have an appointment with my endocrinologist on Saturday, so I won't be there, but Anna can show you around."

"Thanks," Jeffrey said, squeezing my hand under the table.

A quiet morning on the farm with Jeffrey sounded nice—and it was—but more than anything, it was busy. They call it the terrible twos for a reason. Asher wasn't bad, but he was into everything, constantly on the go. Before we even got to the cows he spotted Tabitha, one of the barn cats, and of course he had to see her. There were five cats in all, and Tabitha was the friendliest of the bunch. She came right up to Asher, rubbing her gold-and-tan body against his legs. Asher squealed when he touched her.

"Meow! Meow!" he cried.

I chuckled. "That's Tabitha," I told him.

Next he spotted Charlotte, the gray cat, who was more standoffish. Chasing her brought us to Mo, the calico kitty. Mo gave Asher a few seconds of contact and then he darted away, but that was okay because by then Asher had noticed the chickens and he took off after them. The little guy had us bouncing all over the place. After he had his fill with the chicks, I took his hand and guided him to the calf pen.

"Moo!" he squealed in delight. "Moo!"

Jeffrey and I giggled.

"That calf right there was just born last week," I told Asher. "Can you believe you're older than her?"

He looked at me with big curious eyes. I could almost see his brain trying to make sense of everything I was telling him. He was soaking up the information like Mr. Terupt had said young minds do.

"Baby," he said, pointing to the calf.

"That's right." I nodded.

"Baby!" he hollered, sticking his hand through the fence and pointing.

The calf stared back at us. "She's looking at you," I whispered. Asher held his breath. Slowly, the calf approached. "She's coming to see you." Asher stayed perfectly still and perfectly quiet until the calf pressed her wet nose against his hand and snorted.

"Ahh!" he squealed.

The calf jumped and bounded away and Jeffrey and I burst into laughter.

"Nose me," Asher giggled. "Nose me!"

"She nosed you, buddy," Jeffrey said, looking at me and laughing more.

"I thought I heard somebody out here," a voice behind us said. It was Charlie. He was coming from the barn, carrying a couple of pails of milk.

"Hi, Charlie," Jeffrey said.

Charlie nodded. "And what's your name?" he asked Asher after setting his pails on the ground.

"Asher," Asher announced.

"Hi, Asher. I'm Charlie. Are you keeping an eye on my calves for me?"

Asher nodded.

"He wanted to come see the cows," Jeffrey explained.

"Would you like to help me feed them?" Charlie asked.

Asher's eyes grew wide.

"Maybe Jeffrey can help you," Charlie suggested.

Charlie poured some of the milk from the big pail into a smaller pail. Then he opened the gate and led Jeffrey and Asher inside. The calves knew what was happening and came trotting over right away. Asher hid behind Jeffrey.

"It's okay, Asher," Charlie promised, trying to reassure him. Charlie held the pail in front of one of the calves and the cow stuck her head inside and started guzzling. Charlie handed the pail to Jeffrey. "Hold tight," he said.

Charlie handed me the second pail and I fed one of the other calves. For the newborn, Charlie made a bottle and put a nipple on the top. He had to feed her like a baby because she was still that young. Once he had her eating, Charlie coaxed Asher over to help him hold the bottle.

Jeffrey's calf finished first, and when she reached the bottom of the pail she threw her nose in the air and sent the pail flying. Then she jumped and bounded away, full of energy after filling her belly.

The burst of excitement scared Asher, but Charlie held

him close. Jeffrey was equally startled, which was too funny. I'd forgotten how little he knew about the cows. I tried, but I couldn't stifle my laughter.

"Forgot to warn you about that," Charlie said, glancing at me and smirking. That just made me laugh more.

Charlie was great and I was being stupid, that was all there was to it. I was mad at myself for the way I'd been feeling.

"What's wrong?" Jeffrey asked, noticing I'd grown quiet after Charlie went back into the barn.

"Nothing," I said.

"You're sure?" he double-checked, sensing something.

I nodded.

"Okay," he said. "You can tell me whenever you're ready. I'll be here."

Foolish me believed him. Mom wasn't the only one to abandon me.

Danielle

My insulin pump arrived shortly after the start of school, but I couldn't use it until I attended a training session with Nurse Carol, my diabetes educator. The training session was a three-hour one-on-one class with Nurse Carol where I was supposed to learn everything I needed to know about my pump.

But what if I didn't? What if I goofed something up? I was scared and excited and nervous all wrapped in one. I had God working overtime with all the praying I'd been doing, asking Him to help me master this.

"Good morning," Nurse Carol said, greeting Mom and me when we got there.

"Good morning," Mom replied.

"Today's an exciting milestone, Danielle. No more daily shots after this. Are you ready?"

I nodded because I couldn't speak. My throat had gone dry.

Nurse Carol brought us into one of the meeting rooms and we sat around a table. "We have a lot to go over, and it's going to seem overwhelming at first, but we'll take it slow and spend as much time as you need so that you both feel comfortable," she explained. "Ask as many questions as you want."

Mom nodded this time. Was she feeling like me?

Nurse Carol got started. She went over all the parts and supplies associated with my pump, giving everything a name. Then she showed me how to set it up and how to program it. There was a lot to that part. After that, I learned how to put it on and how to actually use it.

It's hard to explain all the intricacies of my pump, but basically I have this thing called an infusion set. That sounds fancy, but it's really just a mini-syringe (full of enough insulin to last me for about three days) with a short length of tubing connected to a tiny needle that is inserted into my arm or belly or leg, wherever I prefer. The spot where I insert the infusion set is called my "site." That's it. Thanks to my pump, I went from seven or eight needle sticks a day to one tiny needle every two or three days. It was way better. That did make me smile.

Nurse Carol had a piece of brown foam that she had me strap onto my arm so I could practice inserting the needle into a site. Mom also practiced so she could help me if I ever needed it. After we did a few trials with the foam arm,

I went ahead and attached my first real pump site onto my left upper arm. Now I was getting a continuous slow drip of insulin—called my "basal rate"—which we spent considerable time calculating when we were programming my pump. The continuous drip of insulin throughout the day was going to help me keep my blood sugars under much tighter control, and that was important in the long run because all those high and low blood sugars did damage to your organs and could lead to long-term problems earlier than for others. This diabetes stuff is serious.

"If you have any questions after you get home or in a few days from now or whenever, there is a one-eight-hundred pump support number you can call, or you can always reach out to me," Nurse Carol said.

I nodded.

"Danielle, you're going to do great," she assured me.

I smiled. Mom and I thanked Nurse Carol and then we left. I felt confident and prepared. Why shouldn't I? We'd gone over everything—almost.

Alexia

It was a big day. Like, super important. I was taking Danielle and Anna dress shopping so they'd have something nice to wear for the wedding. Jessica came too because she was our other bestie, and Danielle and Anna said they wanted her there to add her conservative voice in case I tried talking them into something too risqué. Like I would do that? Whatever. So it was the four of us, but make no mistake about it, I was in charge. I mean, this was shopping we were talking about.

Jessica's mom dropped us off at the mall around one o'clock. We only had the afternoon to find something, which I thought was outrageous, but the girls didn't want to spend all day trying on dresses. Like, what was wrong with them? The mall was heaven.

"Ladies, follow me," I said, marching us into the first

store. With only the afternoon, there was no time to waste. I weaved my way around the racks and quickly determined there was nothing we wanted. "Let's go."

"But we didn't even get to look," Anna protested.

"There's nothing here," I said. "Too boring. Let's go."

"But Danielle and I like boring."

"Not on my watch, you don't. You're not two old ladies. Let's go."

I marched and they followed. It got interesting at our next stop.

"Can I help you find anything?" an older saleswoman asked after greeting us.

"Yes," I replied. "We're looking for a couple of dresses that will accentuate the booty."

"Oh!" the woman gasped.

"You know what I mean. We don't want anything like that," I said, pointing at what the lady was wearing.

"Excuse me?" she said, making a face.

"I'm sorry. That came out wrong. I just mean, like, we don't want anything old and boring."

"I'm afraid we don't have anything for you," the woman snapped.

What was her problem? "Yeah. Well, we don't want any of your granny stuff anyways," I shot back.

"Lexie, let's go," Jessica urged. She gripped my elbow and pulled me away. "C'mon."

"They just lost a customer," I yelled over my shoulder on our way out.

"Maybe we should lead the way while you calm down," Jessica suggested.

"Whatever," I grumbled. But oh my God, as soon as I heard what came out of Anna's mouth next, I knew that was a mistake.

"How about we try Macy's?" she said. "My mom likes that store."

"Absolutely not," I cried. "No offense, but I'm not letting you get a department-store dress."

"Maybe we can just look," Danielle proposed.

"You know what, good idea," Jessica agreed. "There shouldn't be any store workers bothering us in there. Plus, they carry lots of name brands and sometimes you can find good sales."

"Pfft," I scoffed. What did she know? I didn't like it, not one bit, but I let them have their way. "You've got five minutes to peruse the racks," I said, setting clear expectations. "We're not wasting any more time than that."

They jumped right in. Begrudgingly, I decided to look around while they did their perusing. I mean, I couldn't let them shop without me. Incredibly, there was a lot of cute stuff—and for good prices. Danielle and Anna both found dresses that they liked. I wouldn't say they were my style, but they weren't ugly, either.

"Try them on," I encouraged.

"No," Danielle said. "This won't work."

"Why?"

"There's no place for me to hook my pump."

"What do you mean?" Jessica asked.

"I have to be able to hook my pump someplace," Danielle explained, showing us how there was a clip on the back of her pump that slipped onto the waistband of her jeans.

"Can you stuff the pump in your boobs?" I asked.

"What?" Danielle sputtered.

"Seriously, maybe you can tuck it inside your cleavage?"

"My breasts aren't big enough for that."

"Pfft. Whatever! I wish my boobs were half as big as yours!" I exclaimed.

"Lexie, shhh!" Jessica hissed, ducking her head. "Please stop yelling about boobs. You've got everyone within earshot looking at us."

Anna began giggling, and then the four of us burst into laughter.

"Danielle, let me see your pump again," I said after catching my breath. "There must be something we can do to make it work. You can't possibly be the first diabetic who wants to wear a dress."

She unclipped the device and put it in my hand. It wasn't heavy. I looked it over and gave it back to her.

"I'll sew a pocket onto the inside of your dress that can hold your pump for you," I said.

"Really? You can do that?" Danielle asked.

"Yes. And, like, you know I'm gonna make it look legit. No way I'm gonna have my girlfriend looking like anything but the best. If you want that dress, go and try it on."

"Thank you, Lexie." She stepped closer and hugged me.

"You're welcome. Now go try it on," I said.

Danielle and Anna hurried off to the fitting rooms.

"You're a great friend, Lex," Jessica whispered.

"BFFs," I said.

She smiled.

We waited, and a few minutes later Danielle came out modeling a sleeveless navy blue dress with a white floral pattern. Even though it didn't accentuate her booty, it was very pretty and it fit her perfectly.

"That's the one," I said.

"Definitely," Jessica agreed.

Anna appeared next and she looked stunning. Her dress wasn't quite as conservative as Danielle's, but it was far from risqué. We all agreed it would make Grandma talk but not give her a heart attack, so Anna went with it. I'll say this: the girls made a Macy's shopper out of me.

They purchased their dresses and then we went searching for a craft store. Now that Danielle had her dress, I knew exactly what I needed for thread and fabric so I could make her pocket. That turned out to be the easiest part of our shopping expedition, so, like, when we got done there, we still had time to spare, which meant one more stop.

I took the girls to CVS so we could grab a pack of gum and some drinks. They didn't know this, but I also wanted to find nice lipsticks for Danielle and Anna, something that would highlight their lips since we weren't accentuating their booties. Danielle owed me this favor for being her seamstress.

I snuck to the makeup aisle while the girls searched the coolers for drinks. It didn't take me long to find what I was looking for because, like, I'm a pro with lipstick. But when I was sneaking back, something caught my eye that I wasn't looking for—or expecting. It was sitting on an endcap in a case that was supposed to be locked but wasn't. It just sat there staring at me, and it scared me. Like, really truly scared me.

Did I want to know?

october

Jessica

Saving time in a bottle . . .
is what Jim Croce sings about
in a favorite song of my dad's,
who's moving here
from the West Coast
to be
close to me,
and maybe
Mom.

Saving time in a bottle
is what I would've wished for
because I cherished days like those
dress shopping
with my friends.

Saving time in a bottle
is what we're hoping to do with our time capsule.
But capturing the gang and Mr. Terupt
in a bottle
is what I'd wish for,
because
being without one
or the other
scares me.

Peter

It took me all week, but my persistence paid off. I finally found what I was looking for tossed in a recycling bin that was tucked inside the custodian's office. It was the perfect item for our time capsule. I kept it hidden at the bottom of my locker, so I had to run back to grab it before advising, but T wasn't gonna care if I was a few minutes late. It was worth it for a memento like this.

"Better late than never," Lexie remarked when I waltzed in.

"I was looking for something," I said.

"What, your head? Did you try checking in your butt?"

"You know what?" I said, narrowing my eyes at her.

"Okay, you two, let's leave it at that," Mr. T interrupted. "We have a lot on our agenda, and refereeing your boxing match is not one of those things, so cool it."

I took a seat, but not before snarling at Lexie.

"First up is our time capsule," Mr. T said, getting us on track. "Mrs. Terupt found us this lockbox that I thought would be perfect for us to use."

"That is perfect," Luke said.

It was gonna work for what I had, so I was cool with it.

"Who wants to go first?" Mr. T asked. "What did you bring to put in our time capsule?"

"I was hoping to keep mine a secret," I said. "It'll be more fun to open at the end of the year if we don't know what's inside."

"I was thinking the same thing," Jessica agreed.

"Me too," Anna admitted.

"Are any of you opposed to keeping our contributions secret?" T asked.

Everyone was game, so one by one we stashed our things inside the lockbox. It was mysterious and suspenseful and the whole process had us excited to open it. The last person to add his item was Mr. T, but he broke the rules. He claimed his contribution was too good to wait. I didn't see how anything of his could possibly outdo my memento, but I didn't say so.

When he pulled out this black-and-white picture of a white blob, I knew I was right, but then the girls started squealing and freaking out, like it was something great. I didn't get it. I looked harder, but I still didn't get it.

"When is the due date?" Anna asked

"Late May or early June," Mr. T answered.

"What!" I yelled.

"Mrs. Terupt is pregnant," Danielle explained.

"Again?" I cried. "Already!"

T laughed. "Yes," he replied. "Again and already."

"You were just complaining about the cost of daycare for one, and now you're going to have two going? You'll be bankrupt," I said.

"Shut up, Peter," Lexie snapped.

"Is that—" Luke said, pointing to a spot coming off the blob.

"No, I don't think so," T answered, and chuckled. "It's still too early to tell."

"Oh, man! You thought that was the—"

"No way!" Lexie argued, cutting me off. "Hope needs a sister."

I turned to T. "You better make it a boy this time," I demanded.

"Girl!" Lexie shouted.

"What is done is done," T said, "so you two can drop this argument now. Thank you."

Lexie glared at me and I smiled.

"I heard going from one to two is not that bad, but two to three is when it gets nutty," Jeffrey said.

"What do you mean?" Luke asked.

"With two kids, parents can play one-on-one and keep things under control," Jeffrey explained, "but when there's three, the parents are outnumbered and it gets crazy."

"The good news is T will be bankrupt before then," I joked.

"Peter!" everyone yelled.

T just shook his head again. "Sara and I have an appointment with our doctor for an early checkup next week," he said, "so we were hoping to elicit the help of the Babysitters Gang."

"We'll be there," the girls said.

"Don't worry, T. We've got your back," I promised.

"Thanks, gang." He took our time capsule and slid it onto his top shelf as we were leaving. Maybe his picture had sentimental value, but my contribution was still going to be the best.

LUKE

**IF a teacher assigns a long-term project,
THEN the final product had better include
a substantial amount of work.**

Eighth grade was off to a great start. I'd been worried about seeing Mr. Terupt because he wasn't my science teacher, but thanks to advising and the Babysitters Gang, I didn't have to worry anymore.

It was good that things with the gang and Mr. Terupt felt secure because my accelerated classes were a step up from what I was used to. They required more time and energy, but I liked that. I enjoyed the challenge and the learning. I was particularly excited about biology because my teacher, Mrs. Shelley, assigned us a project—a long-term project, to be precise. "Long-term" meaning "not due until after winter break." Initially, I was considering a project on hydroponics or perhaps something with bacteria, but then an unexpected and very different idea came to me during our second meeting of the Babysitters Gang.

Same as last time, we were all eager to report. Mrs. Terupt gave us the rundown on supplies and equipment again, and a few gentle safety reminders. Mr. Terupt left his contact number, and then he took his wife's hand and away they went, off to the doctor for a check on Baby Terupt Number Two.

It was all routine up to that point, but there were two major differences that followed: (1) Hope was awake, not napping, and (2) the girls disappeared. Let me reiterate, Hope was awake and needed watching and the girls were nowhere to be found, leaving us—the guys—in charge. That had to be a safety violation.

Jeffrey got down on the ground near Hope. When I saw that, I decided to sit on the other side of her. Peter chose the couch, where he could keep his distance and work the TV remote. I didn't know if he was scared of the baby or still traumatized from our last visit.

"Don't you want to see Hope?" I asked him.

"I see her. She's on the ground not doing anything."

"Babies are sponges, remember? See how she's studying her elephant and giraffe toys."

"Should I put the tube on Animal Planet? Let her watch some fierce lion kills?" Peter wisecracked.

"How about PBS?" Jeffrey suggested. "*Sesame Street* or *Clifford* would be nice."

Peter groaned, but he changed the channel.

The girls had seemingly vanished, but we didn't need them. We had everything under control—until Hope started fussing.

"What's wrong with her?" Peter asked, sounding panicked.

"Chill," Jeffrey said. "She might just want to sit up."

Peter and I watched in awe as Jeffrey picked Hope up and cradled her in his arms. I was fine sitting near her and reading animal books to her, but not with holding her. Babies were fragile. I didn't want to hurt her.

But Jeffrey got Hope to settle down almost immediately. It was amazing. Who needed the girls when we had him? Unfortunately, it didn't last long. Hope began crying again after only a few minutes.

"What's wrong?" Peter worried. "Why is she crying?"

"Will you chill?" Jeffrey said. "Babies cry. It's okay."

"But why is she crying now?" Peter asked.

"I don't know. Maybe she's getting hungry?"

"Yes, that's it," I said, checking my watch. "Mrs. Terupt said she'd be getting hungry around this time. I remember."

"Where're the girls?" Peter griped. "Aren't they supposed to be helping?"

"Relax," Jeffrey said. "I'll go and heat up her bottle. No biggie. Lukester, you get to hold her while I'm gone."

"Me? But I can't!" I protested.

"Yes, you can," Jeffrey insisted. He placed Hope into my arms and helped to position her so she was comfortable. "She's going to cry," he said, "but that's only because she's hungry, so don't worry. Just hold her and sing or coo to her."

"Who's going to feed her if you can't find the girls?" I croaked.

"Don't look at me," Peter said.

"You can," Jeffrey replied. "It's a heckuva lot easier than feeding a baby cow, I can tell you that."

Jeffrey ran downstairs to the kitchen and I sat there re-playing his words in my head as I hummed softly to Hope. And then it hit me. Suddenly, I had an idea for my long-term project. I'd need to check with Danielle first, but if she had baby cows on the farm, or baby cows on the way, or both, then I could do a really cool study of their growth and development. Height and weight measurements would give me substantial quantitative data, and I could collect more than a month's worth of qualitative observations around behavior.

I glanced at the baby in my arms. Now that Hope had helped inspire my project, I wasn't nearly as scared of her anymore. She was great, and my project was going to be great too!

Scientific inquiry always led to surprises and discoveries. What sorts of surprises and discoveries would I make? I wondered.

Answer: More than I ever imagined.

Alexia

I was tough, but like, I was way too chicken. I could've read the directions and tried doing it myself, but this was some scary stuff. I needed moral support. I mean, this was like telling me my future. So I waited until my BFFs were with me, and as soon as Mr. and Mrs. Teach left, I grabbed Jessica's hand and had the girls follow me to the bathroom.

"Lexie, what're we doing?" Jessica asked. "Hope is upstairs. We can't leave her up there with the guys."

"They're fine," I said. "I need your help."

"With what?" she wanted to know.

"This." I closed the door and pulled out the Gene-Link box.

"Where did you get that?" she pressed.

"I swiped it from CVS when we were at the mall."

"You stole it?!" Danielle cried.

"Quiet," I hissed. "Yes, I stole it. This thing costs like two hundred dollars. I didn't have any choice."

She closed her eyes and began praying. "Dear God, please forgive—"

"What is it?" Anna asked.

"It's a kit that's gonna tell me what's in my DNA, so I'll know if I carry the BRCA1 or BRCA2 genes," I said.

"What are BRCA1 and BRCA2?" Anna asked.

"They're the genes most commonly linked to breast cancer," Jessica answered. "Lexie, are you sure you want to do this?"

"I don't like it," Danielle whined.

"Too bad. You don't have to like it," I said. "You're not doing it. I am."

"Don't you think—"

"Enough with the questions," I snapped. "I'm doing this. Now help me."

The girls glanced at each other but didn't dare say another word. They knew I wasn't messing. Jessica took the box and opened it. "We need Luke for this," she said. "Science is his thing."

"No," I ordered. "He'd never be able to keep his mouth shut about a project like this. We're the only ones who can know. Is that clear?"

They nodded.

"Is that clear?" I repeated, louder this time.

"Yes," they replied.

"Good."

Jessica pulled out the test kit and the directions and started reading.

"What does it say? Like, what do I need to do?" I could feel my heart racing.

"Give me a minute. I'm trying to read," she said. "When was the last time you ate or drank?"

"I don't know. Why?"

"It says you need to wait at least thirty minutes from the last time you ate or drank before doing the test."

"What for? Don't I just pee in this thing or something?" I said, grabbing the tube thingy that came in the box.

"No, you don't just pee in it," Jessica said, mimicking my voice. "You collect your spit in it."

"What? I can't spit that much. That's disgusting."

"Guess you can't do it, then," Danielle said, relieved God was going to bail me out.

I sighed. "How do I do it?"

Jessica took the pieces from the box and put the spit collector together. Then she handed it to me. "Start spitting."

"How much?"

"Up to the line," she said, and pointed. "Not counting any bubbles."

"Ugh," I groaned. She didn't have to be so mean about it. I took a deep breath and then I closed my eyes and spit. Then I spit again. And again. And again.

When I finally finished, I held up the tube. There was

spit dribbling down the side and onto my hand, but I'd done it. "Now what?" I said, feeling exhausted and light-headed.

"Now we seal it inside this package and mail it," Jessica explained.

"That's it?"

"That's it. And then you wait for six to eight weeks to get your results."

"That long?"

"That's what it says," Jessica growled.

"Lexie, please don't open the results on your own," Anna pleaded. "You need to have somebody with you . . . in case," she said, her voice trailing off.

"Yes, Anna's right," Danielle agreed.

"Promise us you won't open the results alone," Jessica demanded.

"Fine. I promise." I was too tired to argue.

Knock knock.

"Are you guys okay?" It was Jeffrey.

I gathered the box and wrappers and my spit package and stuffed everything in my purse. "Not a word," I warned the girls. Then I pulled open the door. "We're fine. Girl stuff. Sounds like you could use help with Hope, though." I stepped past him and headed for the family room.

Now I just needed to drop my spit in the mail—and wait.

Jeffrey

Open mats was the thing I looked forward to more than anything else—even more than advising. At this point, it'd become a routine. Dad and I would pick up Peter and meet Coach Terupt at the high school. Asher usually tagged along. Terupt called him "the next generation." He said Asher was going to be good from the start by virtue of watching his older brother. I smiled when he said that. Wrestling was a family thing now.

After Peter and I put our wrestling shoes on we'd start warming up, jogging around the mats and rolling out our shoulders. Once we were good and loose, we'd grab a partner—mine was always Peter—and begin drilling, which was what we called practicing moves. The way it worked was, I'd hit a certain takedown three times and then Peter would go. Terupt was big on drilling. He made sure Peter and I understood that the best guys were the ones who hit their moves hard—but also correctly—when drilling, and there was absolutely no lollygagging in between reps. You bounced up off the mat and got right back to it.

Coach Terupt promised drilling the right way was going to get us into the best shape and develop us into hard-nosed wrestlers. And he didn't only tell us this stuff, he showed us. First, he grabbed hold of me for a few minutes, and then he did the same with Peter, and boy did we get it after that. Coach Terupt was nasty.

The main thing that was important to remember when drilling was to try to practice all of our moves and different positions that we'd learned at camp and from Terupt, especially the newer techniques.

After we spent time drilling we always moved into scrimmaging. Peter and I did a lot of scrimmaging together because there weren't always other kids our size who we could wrestle with. Freddy didn't always come to open mats, but when he did show up he liked to go with me.

"He likes beating you," Dad had said on our way home after the last time I'd wrestled Freddy.

It was true. I did okay against him on our feet, but when he got on top he killed me. He used his legs and tied me up and I didn't know how to stop him—until Coach Terupt spent thirty minutes going over that position with Peter and me at our next workout. Peter and I had drilled the different moves every practice since, so when Freddy showed up the next time it was a different story. I didn't beat him, but I'd closed the gap. Freddy stormed out of practice that night.

"Iron sharpens iron," Coach Terupt told Peter and me. "You're lucky you've got each other. Be coachable and keep working hard to get better. Good things will happen."

I glanced at Peter—my drill partner and best friend. We fist bumped. It would've been cool if Peter could move to varsity with me, but he was 113, and 113 was going to be my spot. Nothing was stopping me. Not my best friend. Not anything.

Danielle

After weeks of prayers and planning and preparations, the big day was finally here. Charlie and Terri were exchanging vows and becoming husband and wife. God gave us a beautiful afternoon, with clear blue skies, a gentle breeze, and just-right temperatures. Everything about the day was perfect. Everything except for the thing I didn't want to tell anyone. I didn't want to ruin perfect.

Guests for the wedding parked at our farm. From there they climbed aboard a wagon that was hitched to one of our tractors driven by my father. Imagine a hay wagon ride, but instead of hay bales, Charlie and Dad and Grandpa had built benches for the passengers to sit on. Mom and Grandma did their part and made sure the seats were cushioned and covered with nice cloth.

Dad drove slowly and carefully, but the ride out to the

ridge was still a bit bumpy. After all, we were on a wagon riding across pastures. But it was fun. People seemed to enjoy the ride. At least, no one complained, especially me—not even after my pump site ripped off.

It happened so fast that no one saw it. Lexie's pocket held my pump for me, but the tubing still had to travel to my site, which I had on the back of my arm. Had it been on my leg this never would've happened, but the little bit of tubing coming out of my dress at my armpit caught on the wagon railing after one of the bumps—and that was all it took. Simple as that. I barely felt it—but I knew.

Without my site attached there was no insulin being delivered to my body. Not an immediate emergency, but without insulin my blood sugars would begin rising within fifteen minutes—and they'd continue rising. My dad's words came back to me. *The last thing any of us is going to do is ruin this wedding. Is that clear?*

I needed a new site as soon as possible—but I didn't have any pump supplies with me. Did Nurse Carol mention to always have an extra set with me for emergencies like this? I couldn't remember, but where was I supposed to keep all that stuff anyways? Lexie's pocket wasn't a storage closet. It took care of my pump and that was it. One thing was certain: I wasn't about to ruin my brother's wedding by making everyone stop and wait for me to go back to the house to get what I needed—because of my irresponsibility! So instead, I ignored the situation. I never said a word. Made no mention of it. I'd worry about it later.

Following the ceremony, we had the reception, which

was happening in our big barn garage. Grandpa and Dad and Charlie got that ready just like they did the wagon ride. They had moved all the equipment out and swept and cleaned the place spick-and-span, and then the tables and chairs were brought in. The garage wasn't too far from the house, so when there was a break in the action I'd try to slip away and take care of things without anyone noticing. But until then I'd just stick with low-carb foods and keep hydrating and dance a lot to burn the excess sugars. It was a good plan, and it might've worked, but the soda that I thought was diet wasn't. My sugars went through the roof. And then it turned from bad to worse.

ANNA

The way Lexie screamed and carried on after getting stung by that jellyfish absolutely made it feel like a matter of life or death, but the true life-or-death scenario happened at the wedding.

The last thing Danielle wanted was to ruin Mom and Charlie's day, so she never said a word—not even to me. I had no idea about her failed site or the extreme danger she was putting herself in. She made it through the ceremony and gave it her best try at the reception, but there wasn't a person alive who could've kept going in her condition.

I missed all of the early signs—the way she kept guzzling those pitchers of supposed-to-be-diet soda, the fact that she didn't eat and had to go pee multiple times. I took all sorts of pictures, but never saw how sick and pale my best friend was until I looked back. I should've recognized something was wrong, but I didn't—not until it was too late.

When Danielle didn't return from the bathroom on one of her many trips, I went searching for her. I found her lying in the fetal position near the toilet, clutching her belly in pain. The place reeked of vomit.

I ran to get Mrs. Roberts and Grandma. Danielle tried explaining about her failed site, but she wasn't making complete sense. Mrs. Roberts spotted Danielle's blood-testing kit resting on the sink and used it to prick Danielle's finger. Her sugars were so high the meter didn't even give a number. It read HIGH. How long had she been like this?

"Anna, there's insulin in the house inside the refrigerator. It's on the door. Needles are in the cabinet above the sink. We've got to get her to the emergency room, but she needs a shot now."

I didn't ask questions, though I had many. I sprinted out the back of the garage and found everything Mrs. Roberts needed. We tried our best to handle the situation without making a fuss. Things at the reception were going well, and Mom and Charlie were supposed to take off for their honeymoon weekend on Cape Cod afterwards, but once they saw what was happening, that changed. They insisted they were going to the hospital too. They said their honeymoon could wait. I started crying.

"Anna!" Mom said, pulling me into a hug. "It's okay. The doctors will help Danielle get better."

"I'm supposed to be her best friend. Her sister," I sobbed into Mom's shoulder.

"You're those things and more," Mom assured me. "This wasn't your fault or Danielle's or anyone's. We just need to get her help."

I nodded against Mom's chest. There was so much I wanted to say, but I held my words.

"I'm going to run inside the house and change and then we can go."

"I'm sorry this happened on your wedding day," I mumbled.

Mom squeezed me. "It's okay, honey."

I hugged her tight and then I let go.

It was a good thing Mrs. Roberts insisted on taking Danielle to the hospital, because she was in ketoacidosis. The doctor might as well have been talking in another language when he said that word, but he explained. If I was Luke I would've understood everything he told us, but that wasn't the case. I got the big picture, though. This was serious.

"I'm sorry," Danielle croaked after the doctor left the room. Her voice broke and then she began crying.

"You don't have to be sorry," her mother said, comforting her.

"But I'm supposed to be responsible."

"You are," Grandma insisted. "This diabetes stuff is a lot for anyone to remember. You'll learn from this and next time you'll have an extra set of supplies with you—because you are responsible. So stop this feeling-sorry-for-yourself nonsense."

"Danielle, I'm going to help you remember," I said. "Being a diabetic is a twenty-four seven job, but so is being your best friend–slash–sort of–sister now."

She smiled—and then so did everyone else.

"You know, Danielle, I'm beginning to think you should be a softball player," Charlie teased. "After all, you're batting a thousand. Last year you goofed up Christmas Eve *and* Christmas, and now you messed up my wedding day."

Mom punched Charlie in the shoulder and he winked at us. The room broke into laughter, Danielle included. I was happy for Mom and Charlie, but I couldn't change how I was feeling. I wished a little insulin could've fixed me like it could Danielle, but inside I was only getting worse.

november

LUKE

IF I collected enough data,
THEN I would have an excellent project in the end.

Collecting data required site visits, meaning trips to Danielle's farm. And this wasn't the sort of thing that I could put off, because the baby cows weren't going to wait to grow. The good news was I didn't have to go it alone my first time. The gang came with me because everyone wanted to check in on Danielle. She'd missed school earlier this week after she ended up in the hospital over the weekend thanks to her diabetes. And then we didn't have school on Thursday or Friday because of a power outage, so none of us—minus Anna—had seen her.

According to Anna, Danielle's pump site had fallen off

before the wedding, so she went several hours without insulin. The result: Her blood sugars skyrocketed.

IF Danielle's sugars stay excessively high for too long, THEN the result will be ketoacidosis.

Anna couldn't explain the first thing about ketoacidosis, commonly referred to as DKA, but that was okay because I already knew about it. To simplify, when blood sugars stay elevated for too long, your blood can become acidic. I could explain the science behind that but it gets complicated. Just think about your blood turning into acid and you get the point. Not good. Danielle was lucky.

Anxious to get to work on my biology project, I was the first to arrive at Danielle's, unless you counted Anna. She was already inside, but she practically lived there. Jessica and Lexie pulled in right behind me, and then Peter and Jeffrey got there, so we all approached the house together.

"How are you?" Jessica asked the moment Danielle opened the door.

"Are you okay?" Lexie asked before Danielle could even respond.

"Did you almost die?" Peter shouted from behind us.

Danielle chuckled. "No, I didn't almost die. I'm fine."

Her smile and small laugh made us feel better.

"Back in the old days you would've been a goner," I told her. "Before scientists understood diabetes and before we had artificial insulin to give to somebody with a bad pancreas, diabetes would kill you dead."

"Kill you dead?" Peter repeated. "Way to go, Einstein."

"Thanks for coming," Danielle said. "I missed you guys."

"Danielle, don't make your friends stay outside," her grandmother hollered from somewhere inside the house. "I've got fresh cookies waiting for them."

"Fresh cookies?" Peter repeated. "Yeah, let us in."

Cookies did sound good, but I couldn't spend too long socializing. There was no time for procrastinating. I needed to see the cows and get to work on my project.

We kicked our shoes off by the door and padded into the kitchen, where it smelled like heaven. Danielle's grandmother had baked warm oatmeal and molasses cookies. We each grabbed one or two and dug in—all of us except for Jeffrey. He had a cookie, but he never took a bite.

"I don't like these flavors, but I don't want to be rude," he whispered, sliding his cookie across the table to me.

I nodded, helping him conceal the truth—which I never would've done had I known the real truth.

"Who's here to see the cows?" Mr. Roberts asked, stepping into the kitchen.

Timidly, I raised my hand.

"Anyone else?" he asked.

"Peter and Jeffrey want to join," Lexie answered, volunteering them for the job.

"Good. Let's go, then," Mr. Roberts said, grabbing an oatmeal cookie on his way out.

Peter and Jeffrey sneered at Lexie, but then they followed. I was happy to have them tagging along.

Mr. Roberts paused at the door. "One of you can put on

Charlie's galoshes, unless you don't mind getting cow poop on your sneakers? You might want to think about getting yourselves some boots if you're going to be coming here again, though."

Note to self: **IF I don't want cow poop on my sneakers, THEN I should get barn boots.**

Peter shoved past me and grabbed Charlie's galoshes. I was going to put them on since this was my project, but I wasn't going to make a big stink about it right now. Mr. Roberts was waiting, and besides, I needed to get started.

Once Peter was ready, we followed Mr. Roberts out to the calf pen. "These are our newest additions," he said.

I looked. There were two calves. Multiple sets of data. This was even better than I had hoped. I smiled.

"Danielle tells me you're interested in measuring the height and length of the calf," Mr. Roberts continued. "If I was you I'd also measure its girth. Here's a tape measure you can use," he said, handing it to me. "Just don't lose it."

I nodded.

"Wait here. I'll be right back," Mr. Roberts said.

"What the heck is its girth?" Peter whispered after Mr. Roberts had walked far enough away.

"The measurement around its chest and shoulders," I explained.

"You mean you need to wrap the tape around the cow?"

Again, I nodded.

"Good luck with that," Jeffrey snickered.

What did he know that Peter and I didn't?

"Since there's a couple of you, here's what I suggest," Mr. Roberts said after returning with a large bucket of milk and an empty medium-sized black pail. "Each calf gets a black pail full of milk. Fill the pail and then one of you should carry it inside the pen and hold it so that the calf can drink. The calf will stand still while it eats and Luke can use the tape measure to get his measurements."

We nodded. Sounded easy enough, but in the back of my head I remembered Jeffrey telling me feeding Hope was easier.

"I'll check back with you in a few minutes," Mr. Roberts said. "Make sure you hold the pail with two hands" were his parting words.

Jeffrey filled the black pail and then Peter grasped it and walked into the pen. The calves met him at the gate.

"Look out! One at a time!" Peter barked. He tried lowering the pail so a calf could drink from it, but before he could get it down to their level, one of the young cows head-butted the bottom of it and sent the milk flying all over him. "What the heck, you dummy!"

I laughed.

"Yeah, real funny," Peter snapped. "This is your stupid project. You should be feeding these idiots."

"I can't. I've got to use the tape measure, remember?"

"'Gotta use the tape measure,'" he mimicked in a high-pitched voice. "Stupid project."

Jeffrey filled the pail again and this time Peter was ready. He backed into the pen, using his body as a shield to keep the calves away until he had the pail lowered. Then he turned around fast and stuck the pail in front of the nearest calf and she started guzzling. I hurried over and got her measurements.

"Piece of cake," Peter bragged, before realizing the second calf was trying to eat his sweatshirt. Couldn't blame the cow, because he must've smelled and tasted like milk after wearing the first pail. "Get out of here!" Peter yelled, kicking at the sweatshirt eater. That worked, but he should've continued paying attention to the one drinking, because when that calf finished, she lifted her head hard and fast, ramming the pail into Peter's crotch.

"Son of a gun!" he cried. "Right in the family jewels." Peter dropped the pail and fell to his knees, planting his hand in a fresh cow patty.

"Two, takedown!" Jeffrey yelled.

"Stupid cows!" Peter bellowed, shaking his arm. He managed to get back to his feet and then he hobbled to the nearest fence post and leaned against it.

Jeffrey and I roared with laughter. Had I been paying attention to more than just the calves, I might've noticed that this was the first Jeffrey had laughed all day, and then I might've wondered about that—but I didn't give it any thought.

After laughing at Peter, Jeffrey stepped inside the pen and grabbed the black pail and filled it up yet again. He fed the second calf without issue and I was able to get all of her measurements.

"Looks like you boys have had some fun," Mr. Roberts said, rejoining us. He glanced at Peter and smirked.

Peter scowled.

"C'mon," Mr. Roberts said. "I'll show you where you can wash your hands and hose off your clothes."

We followed him, but before we reached the barn, a car pulled into the driveway and parked. A man got out.

"You boys know who that is?" Mr. Roberts asked.

"No," we replied.

"Me neither," he admitted. "Can I help you?" he yelled to the stranger.

"Hi. I'm Jack Writeman. I'm here to pick up Jessica."

anna

"Who's that?" I asked when I saw the strange man getting out of his car in Danielle's driveway.

"I don't know," Mrs. Roberts responded.

"He's a young fella," Grandma replied.

"He's wearing khakis and a sports jacket, so whoever he is he must be smart," Lexie concluded.

"You got all that just from what he's wearing?" I said.

"Absolutely!" she exclaimed. "Now you see why fashion is so important. One look at me when I'm older and people are going to know I'm the queen."

Danielle glanced at me and smirked. "Drama queen, maybe," she whispered.

During our silly banter, Jessica had quietly made her way to the door. She had her shoes on and was getting her jacket before we even realized.

"Hey, where're you going?" Lexie wanted to know.

Jessica froze. She stood there, staring at the floor. Something was wrong. She sighed, slowly raised her chin, and looked at us. "That's my dad."

"What?!" Lexie freaked, unable to control herself. "You mean he's here visiting and, like, you didn't tell us?"

Jessica shrugged while scrunching her face. It was a response that definitely meant "sort of, but not exactly."

"He's not visiting?" I asked, hoping for clarification.

She shook her head.

"What!" Lexie super freaked. "Girl, you best tell us what's going on."

Another sigh. "My dad has moved here," Jessica said.

"Moved here!" Lexie shrieked. "Like 'moved here' as in 'for good'? Like, lives here, moved here?"

Jessica nodded.

"Whoa," Lexie replied, her voice barely above a whisper. She grew quiet as the enormity of what we were learning began to sink in. And then, "I can't believe you didn't tell us!"

"I've gotta go," Jessica said. "I'm glad you're feeling better, Danielle. Thanks for the cookies, Mrs. Roberts." She opened the door and slipped away before we could say anything more.

"Unbelievable," Lexie mumbled.

"She sure dropped a doozy on you, but she'll tell you girls more when she's ready," Grandma said.

Funny thing was, I'd been telling myself the same thing about Jeffrey. I wasn't sure why, but he'd been especially moody this past week in school. I began to wonder if there was something he wasn't telling me. Was it school? Something at home? Wrestling? I didn't know and I was trying not to pry—in case the problem was me.

"She'd better be ready soon," Lexie complained. "Like, real soon. I still can't believe she kept this from us."

"Give her time and space," Mrs. Roberts said. "This is a big change in her life. I'm sure she's experiencing a range of emotions."

Time and space . . . That was all I'd given Mom and she was still no closer. Time and space were exactly what I'd been trying with Jeffrey, and it wasn't working any better. Time and space were the last things I wanted to hear about. I was the one dealing with a range of emotions, and it was getting harder to keep them in check.

Jeffrey

Jessica got in the car with that slick-looking salesman and rode away without so much as a word to us.

"Was that her dad?" Luke asked.

"I don't know, but I'm guessing," I said.

"I thought he was in California," Peter mentioned.

"Looks like he's here now," I replied. "And she didn't seem too happy about it."

"Why?" Luke wondered.

"Why is he here or why isn't she happy about it?" I said.

"Both."

"That I don't know."

"I hope Jessica's okay," Luke said.

"What do you say we go inside and have some more of

those cookies?" Mr. Roberts suggested. "Maybe the women can answer some of your questions."

"You guys go ahead," I said. "My dad is going to be here in a few minutes."

"You sure?" Mr. Roberts asked.

"Yeah. Thanks."

"More for me and Lukester, then," Peter chirped.

I watched them walk inside and then I waited. Truth was, I wanted those cookies, but I'd already cut snacks and desserts out of my diet. That was step one in my plan to drop the weight. I thought it'd be easy, but when you start depriving yourself of something, it's crazy how much you start to want it. The smell of those cookies had my stomach growling earlier.

"C'mon, Dad," I said to myself. I wanted to get home. I was hoping to go for a run before it got dark. Wrestling season started the Monday after Thanksgiving and I wanted to be in tip-top shape—but more than that, I knew the only way I was going to shed the eight pounds was by putting in the extra workouts. As soon as I got down to 113, I could challenge for the varsity spot. It was mine. I wanted it so bad I could taste it.

Dad finally showed up ten minutes later, and he wasn't alone. Asher was with him. And Asher needed to see the cows. I was annoyed with my father for bringing him along, but I took my brother's hand and led him to the calf pen. Dad stayed behind, listening to a story on the car radio.

"There are the cows," I said when we got close. "You saw them. Can we go now?"

"They the babies?" Asher asked.

"Yes, they're the babies."

"Do they has teeth?"

"Yes, they have teeth," I said, "but they won't bite you. They'll suck on your clothes, though. Ask Peter."

"Peter?" Asher repeated.

"Yeah. You know what? On second thought, don't ask Peter. I don't think he likes the cows."

"Why?" Asher asked.

"Long story," I said. "You ready now?"

"Hi, boys," Anna said cheerfully, sneaking up on us from behind.

"Anna!" Asher squealed.

"Hi, buddy," she said, giving him a hug. "I brought you something." She unwrapped the napkin she was holding and showed him what was hidden underneath.

Asher beamed. He took the cookie and bit it.

Anna was all smiles. "I brought one for you too," she said, turning to me.

"How many times do I need to say it? I don't want a cookie!" I snapped.

Anna reeled. I'd scared her. I felt bad—but I couldn't explain.

"C'mon, Asher. We've gotta go," I said.

He waved to Anna and then followed me. Asher was so focused on his cookie that he didn't put up a fuss about leaving the cows. I could've thanked Anna for that, but when I glanced over my shoulder she was already walking the other way. But even with her back to me, I could see she was wiping her face.

I sighed. There was a price that came with being a champion.

Danielle

Luke was the last one left waiting for his ride. The way he kept glancing across the kitchen table and then looking away, I got the feeling he wanted to ask my dad something, but was having a hard time finding the courage to do it. Grandma noticed too.

"You better ask him before he finishes his coffee and you miss your chance," Grandma said.

Dad lowered his newspaper, looking surprised, but not as surprised as Luke. Mom and I grinned. Leave it to Grandma to prod things along. There was no beating around the bush with her.

"You've got a question for me?" Dad asked, lifting his mug and taking a sip of his coffee.

"Yes," Luke croaked. "I was wondering . . . would it be

okay with you if I continued to come over and study the calves? The more data I can collect, the better my project will be in the end, and I'm hoping to get the best grade."

"I don't see why that would be a problem," Dad said. "We feed the calves morning and night, but you can come whenever you'd like. Just do me a favor and make sure somebody knows when you're here, for safety's sake."

Luke's face brightened and his chest swelled with relief. "I can do that," he promised. "Thank you, Mr. Roberts."

"You oughta get Danielle to help you," Grandma suggested. "She spends more time with the calves than anyone else."

That was true, but it still made my cheeks burn. What was Grandma trying to do?

"She'd be a heckuva lot more help than Peter was, I can assure you of that," Dad said, and chuckled. "Have her show you our pregnant cows too," he added before returning to his paper. "You might want to collect data on them as well."

"Yes, I would. I was hoping you had a pregnant one!" Luke exclaimed.

"We've got two of 'em," Dad said. "Danielle will show you. Just be careful."

Luke turned to me, looking like a puppy hoping to go on his walk.

"C'mon," I said, rising from the table and starting toward the door. "Follow me." I sneered at Mom and Grandma and their giggling on my way out of the kitchen.

Luke and I got our stuff on and traipsed out to the barn.

I took him to the holding pen, which was where we kept the cows who were expecting.

"They're the pregnant ones?" Luke asked.

"Yup."

"But how do you know? They look normal."

"Well, one of the first signs is when XT stops paying attention to them," I said.

"XT? Who's that?"

"He's our bull."

"The father?" Luke asked.

I nodded.

"And when a cow is pregnant he ignores her?"

"Pretty much," I said. "He goes after the others instead."

"One bull for all the girl cows?" Luke questioned.

I grinned.

"Huh" was all he could think to say.

"When we start to suspect a cow might be pregnant we keep an eye on her, and once we have a strong sense that she is and she's farther along in her pregnancy, we move her into this pen where we can keep a better eye on her. This is where she'll stay until she delivers. Don't worry, they might look normal to you now, but you'll see changes soon."

"What kind of changes?"

"Well, the cow's belly will start rounding, and her udder will begin filling and stretching, and . . . and her . . . her girl parts will swell too."

"Oh," Luke responded, his eyes getting bigger. "When are these cows due?" he asked.

"Hard to give an exact date, but probably around Christmas, which is why they've been moved here. Cows like to be away from the herd when they're getting ready to deliver."

"You sure know a lot about cows."

I smiled. "I've grown up with them. You should be here to see one of them deliver. That's an experience you'd never forget. I try to be here for all the births."

"That would be amazing!" Luke exclaimed.

"I can call you when I think it's getting close."

"Wow! Thanks, Danielle."

I smiled. "You're welcome."

A horn beeped in the driveway. "That must be your ride," I said.

"Yup. Thanks, Danielle. My project is going to rock."

I waved and he ran back toward the house. When I turned around and started in the other direction, I caught sight of Anna, head down and hurrying away through the rear of the barn. Where had she been? Jeffrey had left a while ago. Did something happen?

ANNA

Jeffrey had me so upset that I just wanted to be left alone, so I hid in the barn. He'd never raised his voice with me before, and he certainly hadn't ever yelled at me, but that's exactly what he did. He'd yelled at me.

I stayed hidden for a while, and then I wiped my face and hurried into the house and upstairs to Charlie's old bedroom. I knew I wouldn't find anyone there now that Charlie had moved in with Mom and me. This was the new guest bedroom, but since I stayed over so often, Mrs. Roberts told me to make it my bedroom away from home. I had some boxes of clothes and personal items that I was unpacking and putting away when Danielle came and found me.

"Anna, is everything okay?" she asked.

"Yes," I lied.

"Are you sure?"

I nodded, but I kept my eyes from her. Lying once was hard enough.

She sighed. "Okay, but just so you know, it's not my farmer instincts telling me otherwise, it's my best-friend-slash-sister instincts. We can talk when you're ready."

I nodded again, and she left. I wondered if she would've gotten me talking if she'd stayed, but she didn't. So we didn't. We never talked about it until it was almost too late.

I reached inside the box I was unpacking and took out a shirt. The same boxes that had been used to move Charlie into my house were helping to move me out, so there was more space for Charlie and Mom—and less for me. I felt so lonely—and the one person who tried talking to me, I'd pushed away.

Alexia

I just couldn't believe that Jessica's dad was moving here and, like, she hadn't told us. Not any of us. I mean, I would've been royally ticked off if she'd told Anna or Danielle and not me, but like, that didn't make it all better. The more I ruminated about her not telling *me*, the madder I got.

By the time Mom finally showed up at Danielle's I was really P.O.'d. Margo was waiting for me in the front seat like a good girl, but not even her cuteness and kisses were enough to calm me down. I must've been radiating anger because Mom felt it.

"You seem upset," she said. "I'm sorry I was late."

"It's fine," I grumbled.

She cast me a sideways glance. "Did something happen?"

"Did something happen?" I scoffed. "You could say that.

I mean, we only learned that Jessica's father has moved here—and like, not because she told us! He was the one who picked her up. Surprise!"

"Oh," Mom said. "Her mother mentioned he was moving to town, but I didn't realize it had already happened."

"Wait, what? You knew? And like, you didn't tell me, either! Oh my God! Don't even try talking to me. You're unbelievable."

"That seems a bit extreme," Mom said.

I gave her the hand. I was done. The rest of our ride was silent.

When we pulled into the driveway, I scooped up Margo and got out, slamming the car door behind me. I stormed into the house, ready to call Jessica and let her have it. No more playing Miss Nice Woman. But when I entered the kitchen, the red blinking light coming from our house phone stopped me. We had a voice message. I played it because, like, I always played them. I didn't want to miss anything.

"Hello. This is Dr. Zou's office, calling to confirm Tiffany Johnson's appointment for this Thursday at one o'clock for a mammogram followed by a PET scan. If you have any questions or need to reschedule, please give us a call back. Thank you and have a nice day."

I looked up. Mom was standing there, staring at me. "Alexia, this is routine stuff. It's nothing to worry about. They do these tests all the time to check and make sure the cancer hasn't come back."

I swallowed. "When do you get the results?"

"I go back in for my checkup one week later."

"I'm going with you."

"You don't—"

"I'm going with you," I said again, cutting her off. Then I turned and walked down the hall and into my bedroom without another word—all for dramatic effect because, like, I was still supposed to be mad at her, but more because I didn't want her to see how worried I was. I plopped onto my bed and got ready to call Jessica, but before I could my phone buzzed. I glanced at the caller ID. It was Peter. Why was he calling me?

"What do you want?" I groaned. He took me from worried back to P.O.'d in record time, another one of his many talents.

"Hey, was that guy Jessica's dad?"

"Oh, you mean you didn't know he was moving here? Welcome to the club because neither did I. Like, can you even believe that?!"

"So that guy was her dad?"

"Yes! And I was about to call Jessica to let her know just what I think when you so rudely interrupted me, so I'm hanging up with you and calling her now."

"Lexie, no! Wait!" he yelled through the receiver.

I huffed. "What now?" I said, exasperated.

"You can't call her when you're this emotional. I can hear it in your voice. You don't want to say something you don't really mean. Something you might regret. I don't know what you saw, but Jessica was in just as much shock as the rest of us when her dad showed up."

I sighed and leaned against my pillows. I hated to admit

it, but like, he was right. Jessica didn't need a crybaby complainer friend right now. She needed somebody ready to listen. She needed the same thing I did. "Peter," I said, my voice low.

"Yeah?"

I didn't say anything. It was quiet.

"What's wrong?"

I took a deep breath, and then I let the words out. "My mom has to go in for tests in a few days, to make sure the cancer hasn't returned. . . . I'm scared."

"Lex, your mom looks great and she hasn't been sick. I'm sure she's gonna be fine."

It was sweet of him to try to reassure me, but the appointment wasn't the only thing scaring me. Mom's tests and results got me thinking about my own—but I couldn't tell him that. "Thanks, Peter."

"Dang."

"What?"

"I was just thinking it's too bad I'm not with you right now because there's probably a good chance you'd want to kiss me, good and long."

"Ugh. Way to ruin it," I groaned, hanging up on him. But then I smiled. He had me feeling better.

Peter was my man, even if he did drive me nuts. Can't live with him; can't live without him. That summed us up.

Jessica

Dad . . .
Showed up.
Surprise!
Thought that would be okay—
it wasn't.
I hadn't told anyone about him,
about his moving here.
Not believing
until seeing.

I have so many questions.
Where are you staying?
How long are you staying?
Is it temporary

or
permanent?
Now what,
Dad?

Mom's only answer is
"We'll see,"
to everything.
How can I explain to my friends
when I only had questions
and no answers?
Too hard,
too complicated.
So instead there was no talking
about him.
No talking
until the gang was together again
at advising with Mr. Terupt.

Talking
is always easier with Mr. Terupt
by our sides.
Lexie goes first,
opening up.

"My mom's test results came back.
She's still cancer-free."
Lexie's body sags

with relief;
mine sags
from guilt.
"I didn't know she was having tests again," I say,
feeling bad—for not being there.
"You've been . . . busy," Lexie says.
But *absent* was what she meant
or should've said.

"It's okay," Lexie whispers,
forgiving me,
or telling me it's my turn now,
or both?

I look at her
with a weak smile and nod,
giving her permission
to ask.

"Is your dad here for good?"
"How can I be sure?" I say,
answering her question with a question.
"He says yes,
but he's broken his promises before.
What's going to stop him from breaking another?"

"It's okay to be scared," Anna says.
I'm terrified.

"IF he moved here, THEN he's serious," Luke adds.
His scientific approach of looking at the facts is
    comforting.
"We'll pray for you," Danielle promises.
So are her prayers.

"Sometimes people need to leave,
maybe forget or get lost for a while,
but they can still find their way home," Mr. Terupt
    says,
giving me hope.

November races by in a blur,
clouded with so many uncertainties,
with Thanksgiving fast approaching
and Dad
wanting to spend it
with us.
We'll see.

Peter

Something weird happened right before Thanksgiving. I got called down to the office. Mr. Lee wanted to see me.

Okay, me getting called down to the office wasn't weird, but it was out of the blue. I hadn't done anything *that* bad, so why was he looking for me? Had the butt prankster struck again? No way. I would've known. Whatever it was, I was innocent, so I wasn't sweating it. I strolled into his office with rap-star swagger.

"Relax, Mr. Jacobs, I didn't call you down here for an interrogation, so you can lose the cool-dude act."

I smirked and took my usual seat. "So if you're not gonna try blaming me for something, what's up?"

"I wanted you to know that I reviewed your teachers' comments for this first trimester."

"And?"

"And they're quite good," Mr. Lee said, leaning forward on his desk. "You've been in zero trouble and you're performing admirably in the classroom. Well done, Mr. Jacobs."

"Thanks, I guess." I wasn't sure what else to say.

"You see, I'm not only the bad guy. I pay attention to the good stuff too."

"I told you I was at my best with Mr. T around."

"Yes, I seem to recall you telling me that. But, Mr. Jacobs, maybe it's time you start to consider that your performance is thanks to you and your hard work. I have no doubt that what Mr. Terupt has taught you along the way is helping, but you're the one earning these grades and comments. Take yourself seriously, Mr. Jacobs, because you have the ability to accomplish much."

I sat there stunned. Was he feeling okay? "This is me, Peter Jacobs, you're talking to," I said.

Mr. Lee chuckled. "Yes, I know. And I hope to see him continuing on this trajectory."

"Tra-what?" I stammered.

"Trajectory," Mr. Lee repeated. "This path. I hope to see you continuing on this path. Keep up the strong work, Mr. Jacobs. Now get back to class."

I got up and sauntered toward the door, feeling even cockier than I had before our special meeting.

"Oh, Mr. Jacobs. One more thing," Mr. Lee said, stopping me before I left.

I turned around.

"Good luck this wrestling season."

"Thanks," I said. "It should be awesome. I've got T as my coach."

Jessica

Thankful . . .
Is how you're supposed to feel
at Thanksgiving.
I am.
But more than that
I'm nervous
about having three at our table again
instead of just Mom and me.

How will this go? I worry.
A quiet room with only the sounds of clinking
    silverware and dishes,
a heavy silence with all that is left
unsaid?

Or will there be words?
And what will the words say?
We'll see.

We're taking a big step.
For me?
For Mom?
For Dad?
For us?
We'll see.

But in the end
my nerves and worrying are for naught.
In the end
I'm more thankful
than nervous,
because there are words,
kind and nice,
not about the past—not today.

Today we are thankful
to be three at our table again.

december

LUKE

IF you spend extra time with someone,
THEN one of two outcomes is probable: (1) You grow
apart after getting on each other's nerves, or
(2) you grow closer.

My farm project was off to a tremendous start. I established a schedule where I visited Danielle's farm on Monday and Wednesday afternoons and Friday mornings before school. The morning was tough, especially when it was cold, but I wanted to have a.m. and p.m. data so that I could compare. This was only one of several different data analyses I had planned for my project. Mine was going to be the best. I loved projects, but I was already learning so much with this one that it ranked right up there with the best Mr. Terupt projects.

Usually, I preferred working alone on assignments of this magnitude, but Danielle was a terrific assistant and an exceptional resource. She was there to help me on every one of my visits, even on the cold mornings.

One of the first things I noticed was how comfortable the calves were with Danielle. They weren't nearly as jittery around her as they had been with Peter. They still sucked at her shirt and head-butted the milk pail, but she was used to it and didn't go berserk like Peter had. I wasn't sure if you'd ever call a calf a pet, but Danielle had that kind of relationship with them. It made getting my measurements a piece of cake.

"The calves trust you," I said.

"The more you're with them, the more comfortable they'll grow with you too," she assured me.

"In my research, I read somewhere that cows are a reliable judge of character. I can see why they like you." I meant that, the last part especially, but I didn't mean to say it out loud. It slipped.

Danielle blushed and giggled. I had to look away.

"You read that somewhere?" she said. "That's funny. My dad always says that."

Come to think of it, now I remembered it was Jessica who'd told me something similar about cows, after she'd read it in one of her books. Jessica, I thought. What was wrong with me? I needed to focus.

"Can we check on the pregnant cows?" I asked, kicking at the ground. I couldn't look at Danielle yet, but standing there in awkward silence was just that—awkward.

Danielle led the way. It didn't take long to reach the holding pen, and the change in scenery gave us something new to talk about.

"Suzie's getting ready," Danielle said, pointing at the light brown cow.

"How do you know?"

"Look," she urged.

I leaned against the fence railing and studied the animal. "Whoa . . . yup . . . it sure looks that way," I agreed, remembering what Danielle had told me about swollen parts.

Danielle giggled. She knew what observation I'd made. Now it was my turn to blush.

"Do you also see how her udder is beginning to stretch?" Danielle noted.

I nodded and jotted those observations in my notebook. I might've been the smartest in the classroom, but out here Danielle was the best. I continued recording notes and observations. I was done after a few minutes, but I didn't say so. I wasn't in any rush to leave.

anna

I'd been careful around Jeffrey ever since he'd snapped at me over a silly cookie. I still hadn't told anyone what had happened—not even Danielle. I was tired of giving him time and space but I didn't know what else to do. I kept hoping he'd come back around. Apologize. But he never did. Instead, he seemed to be pulling away. And it only got worse after wrestling started. We sat with the gang at lunch, but Jeffrey was quiet. And most days he left early. Waiting wasn't going to work, so I tried talking to him about it, but that was a mistake—not my biggest mistake, though.

"Everything okay?" I asked after following him out of the cafeteria.

"Yeah," he answered. Nothing more.

"Wrestling going okay?" I asked.

"Yeah."

"Anything wrong?"

"No!" he yelled. "So stop pushing."

I flinched. That was twice he'd exploded at me now. The instances were weeks apart, but the hurt was no less. I tried not to be too sensitive, but it was hard to hide my feelings after that. I turned and walked away before he could see my eyes watering.

I spotted Danielle down the hall at her locker and started toward her, but as I got closer, I saw that she was busy laughing with Luke. I couldn't bring myself to talk to her—not now.

I was good at helping other people with their problems, but not at dealing with my own. Maybe Jeffrey and I were too similar.

Peter

Wrestling season was officially under way, and I couldn't have been more excited. This season was going to be the best. Jeffrey and I were way more experienced. We'd gone to our second summer camp and had spent the fall going to open mats—and we had Coach T! With him in our corner, we were going to crush everybody—and that was exactly how it went in the beginning. But then the unexpected happened.

Our first two meets were on the road, and Jeffrey and I both won easily. Our third match had us pitted against a better squad, the Madison Tigers. We were finally wrestling at home and we had a decent crowd. I couldn't wait to put my hard work on display in front of my parents and Lexie. Jessica and Anna were in the bleachers too, but Luke and

Danielle were going to miss me kicking butt because they were busy studying cows for Lukester's project. You didn't mess with Luke when it came to school. I wasn't mad, but they felt bad and promised to come when they could, which was cool.

That day's lineup had me wrestling in the fourth bout against some kid named Hogan. There were three seventh graders on our team who went before me. One of them, Louie, rallied to win on a last-second reversal that sent the crowd into a frenzy and really got me psyched before taking the mat.

My match went just the way I'd visualized. I scored three takedowns in the first period and built a 6–2 lead. I started on bottom in the second period and after a quick escape and another slick single-leg takedown, I cranked Hogan over with a tough arm bar and glued his shoulders to the mat. It was my third pin in as many matches.

I glanced into the stands when the referee raised my arm and saw my parents clapping and Lexie smiling. She was the kind of girl who'd want a boyfriend who was good. Well, she had one.

Jeffrey stepped onto the mat next against someone named Oliver. I'd never heard of the kid, not that it mattered. I expected Jeffrey to make quick work of him—but that was not how it went. Jeffrey got in on an early shot but he couldn't finish it. Oliver fought off the attack and then surprised everyone when he spun behind Jeffrey for the first takedown. I hardly ever got a takedown on Jeffrey in practice, but I wasn't worried. Jeffrey would reverse this bum and crush him soon enough—or not.

It wasn't until I saw Jeffrey having a hard time getting away that I started to get a little worried. It took him close to a minute to finally get an escape—and he was lucky he did. The period ended with Jeffrey losing 2–1. The gym went from loud and energized to eerily quiet.

"Let's go, Jeffrey! This is your period!" I cheered, getting behind him.

Coach T and the rest of the guys yelled encouragement too. We were beginning to sense that he needed it.

Jeffrey chose to start the second period in the down position, and once again he had to work hard to get away, but he managed an escape with about thirty seconds to go, tying the score at 2–2. Ordinarily, this was when Jeffrey picked up the pace. Ordinarily. But he was barely moving. He looked tired and his opponent didn't. Oliver went after Jeffrey, firing one takedown attempt, and then another, and then another. Jeffrey got warned for stalling when he backed out of bounds.

"Jeffrey, let's go!" I yelled. This wasn't like him, and I was getting mad.

"C'mon, Jeffrey! You've got this!" the guys cheered.

Jeffrey and Oliver went back to the middle for the restart, and with ten seconds left in the period Jeffrey hit a sick duck under on the edge of the mat and scored a huge takedown to go up 4–2—but this match was far from over. Oliver chose bottom in the last period and Jeffrey kept him down as long as he could, but the Madison Tiger got free and wasted no time in scoring a go-ahead takedown with a nice single-leg of his own. Jeffrey trailed 5–4. Suffering from shock and disbelief, our side of the gym turned silent. Soon the desperate pleas began.

"C'mon, Jeffrey!" Jessica cried. "You can do it!"

"You can do it, Jeffrey!" Anna echoed.

"Jeffrey, move!" I hollered. Now I was angry. He was way better than this.

They rolled out of bounds with twenty seconds to go and Jeffrey came up with a bloody nose. I grabbed the nose plugs from inside our med kit and ran to the corner where Coach T had Jeffrey standing with his head tipped back.

"I know you don't feel well, but you've worked too hard to lose this match," Coach T said, stuffing the cotton into Jeffrey's nose. "Forget about everything else. You've got to focus on the next twenty seconds and score. This is when you win on mental toughness."

Jeffrey nodded and turned to go back to the center. "Let's go, Jeffrey! You've got this!" I shouted.

Jeffrey got set in the down position and Oliver lined up on top. The referee blew his whistle and Jeffrey exploded to his feet, but Oliver was ready and brought him back to the mat. Jeffrey didn't stop. He stood up again, and when Oliver pushed into him and drove him forward, Jeffrey fell to his hands and hit a beautiful switch on the way down— exactly how Coach T had taught us. Exactly how we had drilled it all fall during open mats. Jeffrey got the separation he needed and scooted around behind Oliver. The referee awarded two points for a reversal at the final buzzer. Jeffrey had escaped with a narrow 6–5 win.

Our crowd went crazy. It was an exciting finish, but Jeffrey was lucky. He wrestled like garbage and he knew it. Our parents and friends might've been celebrating—but he wasn't. I knew Jeffrey was pissed—and he should've been, after that performance—so I kept my distance and left him alone. Too bad not everyone knew enough to do that. Still, I'll admit, I didn't know how pissed he was until later.

When the meet was over I spent a few minutes talking to my parents, and as soon as they left and I was alone, Lexie came storming up to me. "If you ever even try to dump me because of some dumb wrestling match I'll knock your lights out," she promised, shaking her fist in my face.

"What're you talking about?" I said.

"Jeffrey just broke up with Anna. He tried saying his wrestling was suffering because of her. Apparently, she's too much of a distraction. More like he's too much of a jerk. I oughta punch you," she growled.

"Me? I didn't do anything," I argued.

"That's right. You didn't do anything. Just let your stupid buddy dump the sweetest girl in the whole world—and for no good reason. You're a jerk." Lexie spun around and stomped away.

I stood there with my jaw on the floor. Jeffrey breaks up with Anna, and somehow that made me the jerk? How in the world? I couldn't win with Lexie.

I gathered my sweats and the rest of my clothes from the bench area and went into the locker room. I looked around for Jeffrey but he wasn't in there.

"Did you see Jeffrey?" I asked Coach T.

"Yeah. I talked to him."

"He's pretty upset, huh?"

"He had a bad match. It happens. He said he wasn't feeling well." Coach T shrugged. "When you wrestle your worst match and still win, that's a good sign."

I nodded. That made sense. But what we didn't know was that we still hadn't seen Jeffrey's worst.

"On the other hand, you looked great out there," T said.

"Thanks."

"Keep working hard, Peter. And don't worry about Jeffrey. He'll come around."

It wasn't often that Mr. T was wrong about something.

Alexia

This was even worse than a bad hair day. I mean, Anna was the nicest, sweetest girl in the whole wide world, and like, Jeffrey goes and breaks her heart because he didn't do well in his dumb wrestling match. Like that was supposed to be her fault. Pfft. Whatever.

"He's gonna come crawling back," I promised Anna, "and when he does, you better not make it easy. You make him work for it. Make him beg and plead."

She sniffled and shrugged.

"You know what? On second thought, when he comes crawling back, send him to me. I'll rip him a new one. He needs to know what an—"

"Okay, Lexie," Jessica said, cutting me off. "We get it. But your anger isn't helping right now."

I huffed, and then, like, Anna started tearing up again. She was in rough shape. Jess and I hugged her. Danielle wasn't there, so it was up to us to try to comfort her. We did our best—but we couldn't fix what Jeffrey had broken.

When Vincent finally arrived, the three of us hurried out to his car. We needed to get Anna away from there.

"How'd everything go?" Vincent asked when we opened the back door and climbed inside.

"Terrible," I snapped. "Guys are stupid, so don't even try talking to us."

Vincent glanced at me in the rearview mirror and smirked. He knew I was serious but that I was also joking with him. He was the best. All this stuff with Jessica and her dad just reminded me how lucky Mom and I were to have him.

We gave Anna a ride to Danielle's because that was where she wanted to go. Jessica and I told her to call or text if she needed anything, but like, I was hoping Danielle could use her praying powers to make things better.

ᴏɴɴᴏ

I had Vincent drop me off at the farm because nobody was home at my place. Charlie was busy with the evening milking and Mom had somewhere she needed to be. I decided to walk through the barn before going inside the house. The cows had a way of making me feel better. Their easygoing nature had a calming effect on me. Charlie said that was because the cows liked me and trusted me. It was more than I could say about Jeffrey.

"Hi, Anna," Mr. Roberts said when he saw me coming through. I was surprised to find him doing chores instead of Charlie, but I didn't say anything.

"Hi, Mr. Roberts." I petted the cow near me.

"Danielle and Luke are out by the holding pen, keeping an eye on Suzie. Looks like she's getting closer to dropping her calf."

"Okay," I said. "Thanks."

I headed in that direction, but when I saw Danielle and Luke hunched together, giggling and having fun, I turned and went the other way. I slipped into the house without Mrs. Roberts or Grandma noticing me and went up to Danielle's bedroom. I didn't want to bother her. She was busy helping Luke. She didn't have time for me right now. Mom didn't have time for me. Jeffrey didn't have time.

I fought the knot in my throat and wiped my eyes. I sat on Danielle's bed and opened a book. I chose her room because my guest bedroom was still too empty and lonely and I didn't need any help with feeling more of that. I read, but I couldn't tell you what I'd read because my mind was elsewhere. I wished I had homework to keep me busy, but I'd finished the little bit I had before the wrestling match.

"Anna!" Danielle said, surprised when she found me in her room. "I didn't know you were up here."

"You and Luke were busy. I didn't want to bother you."

"We were observing Suzie. She's definitely getting closer to having her calf. Luke wants me to call him if I see any activity." She giggled. "He's so excited."

Danielle sat on the foot of the bed and began brushing her hair. "Everything about the farm is so brand-new to him." She giggled again. "He's like a little kid."

I eyed her suspiciously. She stared at the floor, lost in space as she pulled the brush through her hair over and over. Did she have feelings for Luke? No way. Just the thought made the knot in my throat tighten. I couldn't talk to her about it—not now. I hid behind my book.

Danielle never noticed. Mindlessly, she rambled on and on about Luke and his project. She barely stopped talking, but she never asked about the match—or me. She didn't have time for me. There were no best-friend-slash-sister instincts working for her today. She was feeling something else.

Jeffrey

I tried running more and eating healthy for three weeks, and I only dropped two pounds. That plan wasn't going to get me to 113 fast enough, so I started eating and drinking less. In one week's time I lost three more pounds, but I was miserable.

Anna didn't deserve that. I did her a favor. I wasn't in the mood to be any kind of boyfriend, but even so, I wasn't planning on dumping her. My match against Oliver had me messed up. I almost lost. I was supposed to trash that kid. I was supposed to be challenging for the varsity spot. But that was never going to happen with the way I wrestled. I felt weak and exhausted out there. Maybe I was getting sick. That's what my parents and everyone else assumed.

So Mom made chicken noodle soup when we got home. Asher sat at the table, ready to have some with me.

"Ree win. He wessle," he told Mom when she brought the soup out.

"Yes, I know," Mom said. "He did great."

"No, I didn't," I growled.

Mom stopped, startled by my tone. She stood still, holding my bowl.

I pushed back from the table. "I'm not hungry." I got up and went to my room.

"Ree not hungy," I heard Asher saying. "No soup. No no. Ree not hungy."

"No soup," Mom repeated, and sighed.

I lay down on my bed. I felt like garbage, but it wasn't because I was getting sick. It was because I hadn't eaten much. I was down five pounds, but I still had three more to go. The kid I wrestled today wasn't great, but he was bigger and stronger. If I made the weight I'd be against smaller guys. I'd be the bigger and stronger guy. I'd be on varsity, and then things would be better. If I made the weight . . .

Alexia

After dropping Anna off, we went to my house. Jessica was coming over so we could do homework together. We thanked Vincent for the ride when we got there, and then he beeped and drove away, needing to get back to the restaurant. Jess and I went inside and put Margo on her leash and walked her to the mailbox so she could tinkle. I was proud of her because she didn't lift her leg in that obnoxious way that boy dogs do, but squatted in a very ladylike manner instead. I grabbed the mail and flipped through it while I waited for her to finish. I froze.

"What is it?" Jessica asked, noticing my reaction.

I swallowed. Slowly, I lifted the envelope and showed her.

She gasped. "I didn't even know you'd sent the test in," she croaked.

I nodded. We walked back into the house without a word. I tossed the mail onto the kitchen table and sank into one of the chairs. I sat there, staring at the GeneLink envelope. My results.

"What're you going to do?" Jessica asked.

"I don't know. I'm scared."

"I'm scared too," Jessica said. "You need to wait for your mother."

I nodded. "Yeah," I agreed. I grabbed the envelope and stuffed it into my bag and pulled out my homework, hoping that might distract me. Anything to keep me from thinking about you-know-what.

"How about a snack?" Jessica suggested.

I shrugged. "Okay."

Jessica scrounged around in our refrigerator and came back with a plate of veggies and hummus. Healthy snacks. That was the only thing we had in the house—ever since. Would healthy snacks keep the cancer away if the results said it was in my DNA? I wondered.

Jessica sat down across from me and then, like, she just started talking about her dad. Maybe she wanted to change the subject to keep from thinking about my test results, or maybe she felt like dumping her heavy stuff on me since I'd just done that to her. Either way, I didn't care.

"My dad's looking to buy a house," she said.

"That sounds pretty permanent," I replied.

She nodded. "Yes, but looking and buying are two different things."

"You won't believe it until you see it?"

"I'm just trying to make sure Mom and I don't set ourselves up for another big fall. I'm scared of the results."

Jess reached out and took my hand. We didn't talk results or her father anymore after that. We just sat together, doing homework until her mom came to pick her up.

"Lex, promise me you won't open it on your own," she said.

"Are you crazy? I'm not opening it by myself!" I shrieked.

"Promise me."

"I promise," I said.

"Good, because I really think you need to tell your mom. This isn't something to keep from her."

I nodded. We hugged, and Jess left. Once she was out the door I reached into my backpack and pulled out the Gene-Link envelope. I stared at it—and then I walked into my bedroom and buried it in my underwear drawer.

Telling Mom wasn't the hardest part. The hardest part was deciding if I really wanted to know the results.

Because what if?

Because then what?

Peter

Jeffrey's close match against Oliver served as a wake-up call. I was ready to work even harder, and I expected the same response from Jeffrey. But something was wrong with him.

"Yo, are you okay?" I asked him after practice. "You've been dragging. Do you have mono or something?"

"Mono?" he scoffed.

"Yeah. You know, the kissing disease. Were you sucking face with Anna before you dumped her?"

"No," he growled. "Just not feeling the best. I'll kick it soon."

"I hope so. We've got another match coming up."

"I know. I'll be ready."

I wanted to believe him. I kept telling myself he would turn the corner, but he wasn't. And then he broke.

Coach T had us wrestling in groups of three, round-robin format. Each guy got a number: one, two, or three. Numbers one and two scrimmaged for the first minute. Then one and three had a turn. Then three and two. Then back to one and two, and you kept repeating. We did this a lot, and I barely ever got the best of Jeffrey. I scored on him every once in a while, but usually I couldn't beat him—until the now-infamous practice.

I took Jeffrey down twice during our first minute. And then I did it again during our second and third goes. When you start getting the best of somebody who you don't usually beat, it fills you with extra energy and confidence. It's like a switch gets flipped and you're suddenly better. The opposite happens to the guy who's losing. He starts thinking he's no good. He mentally breaks.

When I took Jeffrey down the next time, I turned him to his back and had him pinned. That had never happened before. When Coach T blew his whistle to signal the end of the minute, I let go and Jeffrey got up and shoved me—hard.

I staggered backward, shocked. And then he came at me again, shoving me up against the wall.

"What the heck?" I yelled.

He pulled back, ready to throw a punch, but Coach T grabbed him first. "Cool it!" T shouted. He dragged Jeffrey to the side and when he loosened his grip Jeffrey yanked his arm free and stormed into the locker room.

"What's his problem?" I said.

"Coach Mills, I need you to run conditioning," T told our assistant. Then he went to the locker room.

I snuck in behind him.

"What's going on?" I heard T ask. "And don't tell me nothing."

No response.

"What's going on?" T pressed. He wasn't letting Jeffrey get away with that crap.

I listened closely, but Jeffrey still wasn't talking. Before words came tears. He broke and started sobbing. What was wrong with him? I crept around the corner, but stayed hidden.

"I've been trying to get down to one thirteen," he choked out, beginning to explain. "I thought if I could do it then I could make varsity."

My eyes bulged. One thirteen! Was he crazy?

"Get on the scale," T ordered.

I walked in. I wasn't worried about hiding anymore. I wanted to see this.

"One fifteen," T said. "And you feel like garbage, don't you? You're weak, you have no energy, and your wrestling is suffering because of it."

Jeffrey shrugged.

"I can't believe I missed this," T said, blaming himself.

"How were you supposed to know?" I said, sticking up for him. "We don't have official weigh-ins for junior high."

"I've been around the sport a long time, Peter. I should've known. I just—"

"I'll be better once I make the weight," Jeffrey argued. "I'll be wrestling smaller guys."

"Oh, yeah? And who told you that?" T scoffed.

Jeffrey shrugged again.

"Who?" T yelled. He was legit mad.

"Freddy," Jeffrey admitted. "He cuts weight and wins."

"Freddy quit," T said. "Bet you didn't know that, did you?"

Jeffrey shook his head.

"Guys who spend all of their time cutting weight never get better at wrestling. Eventually, they burn out and quit. Losing weight is not the answer, especially when your body is growing. You saw Freddy had a bad attitude all fall. I can't believe you tried copying him."

"I wanted to make varsity," Jeffrey said. "That was my goal."

"You still can," T said, "but it's at one twenty, not one thirteen. The spot at one thirteen is Peter's."

"Mine!" I exclaimed.

"Yes, yours. This has been my plan all along, but I wanted to keep you with me for the first part of the season. I'm not done showing you stuff, and I'm almost out of time."

There it was again. Making it sound like the end. "What do you mean, 'out of time'?" I asked.

"Before you go to varsity," T said. "I'm keeping you guys with me for the holiday tournament. You need to wrestle that Oliver kid again when you're feeling better," he told Jeffrey.

Jeffrey cracked a smile. Everything about his mood changed. I knew then that kid was dead meat.

"After that, you both make the move to varsity," T said. "Iron sharpens iron."

Jeffrey and I locked eyes. We didn't say anything because we didn't have to. I had my drill partner back. Everything was good again—until it wasn't.

Jeffrey

I'd spent several weeks being miserable, trying to get down in weight, but it only took me two days to get back to my natural weight, back to feeling good and strong and happy again. Happy, except when around Anna.

Once I started giving my body the fuel it needed, it was instant energy and strength. I felt like Popeye eating his spinach. And all the running I had been doing didn't go to waste. Now that I was doing things right, that extra work started paying off. I could go and go and go.

Coach Terupt had us scrimmaging in groups of three again a few days later. Peter wasn't having a bad practice, and he didn't get worse overnight, but I was feeling it. I took him down four times in the first minute.

"Can you go back to cutting weight?" he joked. "This sucks."

I grabbed his hand and pulled him to his feet.

"Oliver is in for a rude awakening," he said.

I grinned. Yes, he was. Now that Peter and I shared the same goal of making varsity, we were pushing each other every step of the way. And Coach Terupt was right there with us, making sure we never let up. But they weren't the only people behind me.

Terupt had a conversation with my dad and filled him in on everything. Dad knew I was committed and serious because of all the extra work I put in, but he was shocked to hear what I'd been trying with my weight. Terupt assured him that I was okay now, and then he told Dad the plan. I never realized how much energy I'd been using just trying to keep my lower weight a secret until that was no longer the case. I was finally able to put everything I had into getting better and working hard, just the way Coach Terupt had said it should be—and it showed on the mat.

I rolled over my next two opponents in our dual meets and then it was time for my rematch. The Holiday Wrestling Tournament was happening at the end of the month. We were hosting for the second consecutive year because our old coach, Coach Brobur, had volunteered to come out of retirement and run it for the league. All the coaches agreed to that in a heartbeat. Running a tournament is a big undertaking, something not many coaches want to be involved in, especially around the holidays. It required lots of preparation and help, which was why the tournament became our project for December advising, and also why

Terupt recruited Lexie, Jessica, and Anna to assist Coach Brobur at the head table on the day of the event. Luke and Danielle couldn't commit to being there because they were still waiting for one of the cows to deliver her baby, but they promised to be there if the calf happened to come early. That was fine by me, because the only person I needed to show up was Oliver.

Jessica

Signs . . .
Can come in many
  S   s
    h   e
      a p

sIZES
f-o-r-m-s.

Signs
can point to many things.
Like directions
or names
or a boy trying to lose weight.

Jeffrey gave us many signs.
Quiet, lethargic, moody,
skipping lunch,
break/ing Anna's heart.
But we weren't getting the message;
sometimes signs can be missed.

Signs
can be actions.
Like Dad joining us for Christmas,
exchanging small gifts with Mom and me.
Exchanging more nice words with Mom.
We'll see . . .

anna

All I wanted for Christmas was Mom and me back to the way it used to be, but this Christmas was about Mom and Charlie. It said so on the brand-new ornament that Charlie gave Mom. The heart-shaped crystal piece hung front and center on our tree, the words *Our First Christmas* etched just above the image of a husband and wife holding each other. There was no Anna in that picture.

I was in a slightly better mood on the morning of the Holiday Wrestling Tournament because Mom was the one giving me a ride. It wasn't much in terms of quality mother-daughter time, but it was a start. Maybe Santa was late in delivering my Christmas wish? Unfortunately, Mom chose to ask about Jeffrey, which was the last thing I wanted to talk about. I would've skipped the Holiday Wrestling Tournament altogether if Mr. Terupt hadn't needed my help. It was hard seeing Jeffrey back to normal but still wanting nothing to do with me. Of course, I didn't get into any of that with Mom, and luckily I didn't have to dodge her questions for long because we had to make a pit stop at the farm before going to school. Mom needed to drop something off for Mrs. Roberts.

I scooted upstairs to use the bathroom when we got there because I'd forgotten to go at home. I bumped into Danielle on my way out, and that was when things went from slightly better to much worse.

Danielle

"You're quiet today," Luke said. "Do you feel okay? Are your sugars high?"

I groaned. "You're starting to sound like my mother."

"Well, you're quiet."

"I'm cold," I said, cradling my cup of hot chocolate. We'd been sitting on overturned five-gallon pails, waiting and hoping for nearly three hours to see Suzie give birth.

"It's okay if you need to go inside to warm up," Luke said.

"No, I'm fine."

He scooted his pail closer to mine and spread his afghan over my legs. "Maybe if we share our blankets the extra layer will help."

I smiled. "Thanks."

That was sweet of him, but the truth was I wasn't quiet

only because I was cold, but because I was distracted. I kept replaying the events of that morning with Anna in my head.

"Are you excited about the tournament today?" I'd asked her.

"No" was her blunt reply, which surprised me.

"Why?"

"Danielle, in case you haven't noticed . . . Wait, that's right, you haven't noticed because you're so absorbed with Luke and his project. Jeffrey and I aren't together anymore."

"What?" I exclaimed. She was right, I hadn't noticed. "What happened?" I asked, my voice barely above a whisper.

Anna sighed. "It doesn't matter. Have fun with your project today. I've gotta go." And she left.

Yes, I'd been busy with Luke's project, but I wasn't self-absorbed. Was I? *Confused* was how I felt. There were feelings stirring inside of me that had never been there before. I wanted them to go away, but they wouldn't.

anna

When you have your heart broken you hurt so bad you can say things you don't really mean. It's hard not to wallow in self-pity. There's not much that can make you think about something other than yourself. That can help you forget about your own terrible life. But something happened at the Holiday Wrestling Tournament that made me forget.

Jeffrey

Last season's Holiday Wrestling Tournament was a memorable one, but I felt like a caged animal waiting for this year's. It was at last year's tournament that I faced Scott Winshall for the first time. I lost, but I gave him his toughest match in two years. It was that match that proved I was for real.

Going into this year's tournament I was the guy with a target on his back. The buzz was that Oliver was going to beat me. We met in the finals and I put an end to that crazy talk in the first thirty seconds of our match. I got my single-leg, and unlike in our first match, this time I had the strength and energy to finish. I lifted Oliver's leg high into the air and foot-swept his other leg out from under him. He slammed to the mat hard. The crowd gasped. I could've held him down but I let him go so I could do it again—and I did.

I hit another crisp single-leg and when he tried countering I switched off to a double and ran him over to his back. The period ended with me leading 7–1. Oliver knew he was facing a completely different wrestler. I saw it in his eyes. He was already beaten.

I got an early escape to start the second period and scored my third takedown. Oliver put his head in the mat and stopped moving. That was it. He broke mentally. I punched a hard cross-face and wrapped him in a tight cradle, ending the match with a pin.

The real Jeffrey Mahar was back.

anna

I didn't know much about wrestling, but I knew the talk of the tournament was about the big rematch between Jeffrey and that boy from Madison who almost beat him the first time they wrestled. To create even more hype for it, Mr. Brobur scheduled it as the final bout of the tournament. I tried not to be interested by keeping myself busy at the head table. I wasn't even going to watch because it brought back bad memories.

"Part of me would be happy to see Jeffrey lose," Lexie said, "but just a small part, because I'd rather see *you* kick his butt."

"Thanks," I said, faking a smile.

Jessica wrapped an arm around me and gave a quick squeeze. She knew I was having a hard time.

When the big match started I did a good job of not watching—until the crowd erupted. I stole a peek to see what had happened and I couldn't look away after that. Jeffrey made that boy look silly.

"He's a completely different person out there," Jessica said.

Yeah, I thought, but he still isn't the Jeffrey I knew before. While everyone else in the gym clapped and cheered for him and the ref raised his arm in victory, I was stuck thinking that maybe I'd been the problem.

LUKE

"Danielle, look," I urged, trying to keep my voice low so I didn't spook Suzie.

"She's starting," Danielle whispered. "This is it."

"I can't believe it," I said, getting up from my pail and standing at the rail. I was about to witness the miracle of life for the first time. I turned around and reached for Danielle's hand, pulling her up to the fence so that she was next to me. The last girl's hand I'd held was Jessica's, I suddenly remembered, feeling bad—but that was a long time ago, I reassured myself.

Danielle and I stayed there, holding hands and barely breathing, for the entire birth. We watched as the newborn calf's head poked out. Then little by little, Suzie pushed the rest of the calf's body out of hers until it fell free and landed on the ground. Suzie turned around and immediately started licking her baby. That part was super gross, but equally fascinating.

"That was incredible," I said, turning to Danielle. "Thank you."

She smiled, and then looked away. We continued watching Suzie groom her newborn, the mother-child bond on full display. I recorded countless notes in my journal. I was still scribbling away when Danielle said she needed to use the bathroom. I told her to go and she promised not to be gone that long. I continued observing.

IF you want to make the best possible observations,
THEN a closer view will help.

Danielle

I expected to find Luke still hunched over his notebook when I returned. I'd made it quick like I promised. I don't know if he got bored, wanted a better look, or if he was testing some wild hypothesis, but it never even occurred to me to tell him to stay out of the pen.

The moment I saw he was missing, a feeling of doom seized me because I knew. I ran to the rail and searched the pen area. He was in there, carefully circling around Suzie and her newborn calf, continuing to record his notes.

"Luke, don't get any closer!" I warned, but it was too late.

Suzie locked her eyes on him and lowered her head. He was a threat to her baby.

"Get out of there!" I yelled.

Suzie charged.

Luke dropped his notebook and scampered for the nearest exit. He wasn't going to make it.

"Hurry!" I yelled. "Hurry!"

He reached the fence and started climbing, but Suzie was closing in fast. I couldn't watch. I cringed and buried my face in my hands, but that didn't keep me from hearing the loud bang as Suzie rammed into the railing and Luke's scream that followed.

Slowly, I peeked. Luke was on the other side of the fence, sprawled flat on the ground. I rushed over to him.

"Are you okay?"

"I twisted my ankle," he said, and grimaced. "It hurts."

"Stay here," I ordered. "I'll get the four-wheeler."

"You can drive?" he asked. "You're amazing."

I grinned. "Sit still. I'll be right back."

"Don't worry. I'm not going anywhere."

I ran into the house and told Mom and Grandma what had happened. They called Mr. Bennett while I took the four-wheeler and got Luke. When I returned Mom helped me move him inside and onto the couch. Grandma took a bag of frozen peas out of the freezer and put it on Luke's ankle.

"Why did Suzie do that?" he asked. "She's always been so gentle and nice."

"You don't mess with a mother and her baby," Grandma explained. "You won't find anything more protective in all of nature."

He nodded. "I guess so."

"Look at the bright side," I said. "You lived to tell about it."

He chuckled. "I've learned so much. Thank you for helping me, Danielle."

I smiled, but I had to look away again.

A few minutes later Luke's dad knocked on the door and Grandma let him in. After some small talk and explaining exactly what had happened, Mr. Bennett loaded Luke into his car and off they went to the emergency room for X-rays.

"Quite the day," Grandma mused after they'd driven away.

"Yes," I agreed.

"I like that Luke. He's a nice boy," she said.

I nodded, but quickly changed the subject. Grandma was on to me.

"Mom, can you take me to the school since it's not too late? I'd like to help Mr. Terupt with the tournament, and I should tell the rest of the gang about Luke."

"Yes, of course. Let me get my jacket."

Grandma cast me a suspicious glance, but she would have to wait to interrogate me. Thank goodness, because I wasn't quite ready for that. And I definitely wasn't ready for what I saw on the way to school.

anna

Jeffrey's performance won him the tournament's Most Outstanding Wrestler Award. The trophy was almost as tall as Asher. It was one big reminder that he was definitely way better without me. I was ready to get out of there.

"Champion or not, he's still a jerk for what he did to you, Anna," Lexie said. "And like, I've run out of patience waiting for him to apologize. If he doesn't do it by the end of my New Year's Eve party, he's going to be sorry. Sorry because he won't be able to kiss you when the ball drops and sorry because he's gonna have my fist to answer to."

"Guys," Danielle called, running up to us. She was out of breath and looked shaken.

"What's wrong?" Jessica asked. "Where's Luke?"

Before Danielle could answer Mr. Terupt was by our sides. "Did Suzie have her calf?" he asked, excited.

Danielle gave a slight nod but didn't say anything. Something was wrong. I saw it in the way she looked at him. In the way she looked at me. There was something even more wrong than what had happened between us that morning.

Jessica

There was nothing poetic about what happened next.

"So how'd it go? And where's Luke?" Mr. Terupt asked Danielle, glancing around the gym.

Danielle swallowed. "Mr. Terupt," she croaked. "Are you moving?"

He froze.

"Are you moving . . . away?" Danielle asked a second time, her voice shaking. "I saw a For Sale sign in your front yard on my way here."

I stopped breathing.

Mr. Terupt let out a heavy sigh. "You weren't supposed to find out like this."

Alexia

These weren't the results I'd been worried about. This wasn't supposed to happen—Teach moving to be closer to Mrs. Teach's family. What about us?

I couldn't. I ran.

anna

My already broken heart found a way to break again.

Danielle

*D*ear God,
   Please. We can't lose him again.

Jeffrey

The exhilaration of getting my arm raised in victory was nothing compared to the devastation I felt when Jessica told us the news about Terupt after Lexie sprinted out of the gym.

Peter

After all we did to save his butt last year, he was just up and moving like it was no big deal. Moving to be near Mrs. T's family.

We were his family before she was.

LUKE

Even though X-rays confirmed that I only had a sprain, my ankle was still killing me—but all the pain went to my heart when we drove past Mr. Terupt's house on the way home and I saw the sign sitting on his front lawn.

Jessica

Signs
can say many things.
Stop
Yield
or
For Sale,
on my teacher's front lawn.

Never fear
Mr. Terupt will make it better;
he always does.
But how can he
when he's moving . . .

away.

january

ANNA

Danielle wasn't supposed to be at the wrestling tournament, so I had arranged to get a ride home with Lexie. Danielle left with her mother and her own hurt feelings. We never talked about what had happened that morning. We never talked about Mr. Terupt moving. We never talked.

And that wasn't all that never happened. Lexie's big plans for her New Year's Eve bash fell through too. It went without saying, none of us felt like partying or celebrating after learning about Mr. Terupt.

That explains why I was sitting at home on New Year's Eve with Mom and Charlie. Their going-out plans also got canceled because Charlie wasn't feeling the best. So the three of us had a quiet, boring night of watching the ball drop on TV. It wasn't until Mom came into my room to say good night that things got exciting.

I was sitting on my bed with my broken heart and sadness when Mom plopped next to me, all happy-go-lucky, glowing and acting as if all was well.

"Anna, you've been extra quiet all day. Did something happen at the wrestling tournament yesterday?"

That was it. That was all it took. I lost it. I'd been holding on to too much, and it came spilling out in a hot blubbering mess.

"Anna!" Mom cried in alarm. She pulled me close and held me, gently rocking while I sobbed and sobbed. When I'd finally calmed down enough to talk, I began telling her about Jeffrey and then Mr. Terupt's news. It was easier to tell her about those things than it was the jealous feelings I'd been harboring since summer.

"The Jeffrey bit will work itself out in time," Mom said. "That's part of growing up. The Mr. Terupt news is part of life. These things happen, Anna. When people get married and have children, things change. Priorities change. Family dynamics change."

"I know," I croaked. "Our family dynamics have already changed."

"What do you mean?"

I took a deep breath.

"Anna, what do you mean?" Mom asked again.

"It's just different now," I said. "It's been different for a while. You and I haven't had lunch together or a mother-daughter movie night in . . . It just feels like you don't have time for me anymore. I love Charlie, but—"

"Anna, you listen to me. No matter what, no matter how things may seem, I'm always here for you. I promise. But you've got to come to me when you need me, because I won't always know. Life gets busy and I might miss the signs. Communication is key in every relationship. Husband-wife, mother-daughter, sister-sister, sister-brother."

I scowled. Why did she include that last one?

"Do you promise to come to me when you need me?" Mom asked. "Do you promise to communicate?"

I nodded. "I promise."

"Good. Then there's something I need to tell you. I wanted to tell everyone at Christmas, but it's still early and things can happen, so Charlie and I decided to hold off. You need to keep it secret for now."

"Keep what secret? What're you talking about?"

"Anna, I'm pregnant."

Peter

I couldn't tell you if the girls or Luke talked to Mr. T when we returned to school in January, but Jeffrey and I sure didn't. We didn't even talk *about* him. What was there to say? The guy had betrayed us.

When it came time for our first wrestling practice after having learned the news, we just put our heads down and went to work. We drilled harder than we had all year—fueled by anger. Watching us, one would've thought we were having a great workout, but we couldn't wait to get out of there, away from the traitor. As soon as practice ended, we made a beeline for the locker room.

"Jeffrey. Peter," T called, stopping us before we made it. "I need to talk to you for a minute."

Here it comes, I thought. His stupid apology and sob story. I didn't want any of it.

We waited for him to catch up to us, but we still didn't look at him. "I talked to Coach Jennings," T said. "He saw you guys wrestle in the finals at the holiday tournament. He wants you to start practicing with them tomorrow."

"Boy, you can't wait to get rid of us, can you?" I snapped. I couldn't hold my anger inside any longer.

T scowled. "I'm not even going to respond to that. We have advising at the end of the week, and we can talk about it then. Right now, I'm telling you what Coach Jennings said."

My muscles tensed. I clenched my teeth. Jeffrey and I were supposed to make the move to the varsity team together, but what did that stuff even matter anymore? I turned and walked away.

Jeffrey

I stood there after Peter stormed off. I couldn't get myself to move. Terupt could see something was eating at me.

"What is it?" he asked.

I shrugged. "Do you really think we're ready?"

"It doesn't matter what I think, Jeffrey. You're the ones who need to believe it. But yes, I think you're ready."

Thoughts raced through my mind. I'd been angry with Terupt ever since I learned he was moving, but now I was beginning to feel something different.

"What else?" he said, knowing I was hanging on to more.

"It's just . . . I was excited about the thought of going to varsity, but now I know this is my last practice with you . . . and I'm not sure I want to move up anymore."

Coach Terupt blinked. "You know I always have your

best interests in mind, and moving up is what's best for you and Peter. You'll have better practice partners and competition, and that will help you keep getting better."

I nodded.

"I'll swing by the varsity practices when I can, and I'm going to do my best to make it to as many of your matches as possible."

"Okay," I said.

"You just need to promise me one thing."

"What?"

"You're still going to be the hardest worker."

"You can count on that," I said.

LUKE

IF Mr. Terupt moves away,
THEN the gang will fall apart.

That was the last statement I wanted to prove, but the data was already supporting it. The gang hadn't been together since getting walloped by Mr. Terupt's news. I had seen Danielle at the farm—even though I was hobbling around on crutches with my foot in an air cast, my project couldn't wait—and that was when she'd filled me in on what I'd missed at the tournament. It wasn't until our first January advising session that we were all together again.

"How were your holidays?" Mr. Terupt asked, trying to start a conversation.

We responded by staring at the floor and shrugging our shoulders.

He sighed. "Okay, no beating around the bush. Best just to get it out there. Sara and I will be moving after the school year ends—whether our house sells or not."

I'd been thinking we could sneak over and vandalize Mr. Terupt's house to prevent anyone from purchasing it, but if he was going no matter what, then I could forget that idea, which came as a relief.

IF you ever have an idea that sounds like something
Peter could or would contrive,
THEN it's probable you've gone too far.

What we needed was a Luke Idea, not a Peter Idea, but I couldn't come up with anything.

"We're moving," Mr. Terupt repeated. "There's no stopping this one, gang. So please don't try. That'll only make things harder."

"But why?" Lexie croaked. "I thought you liked it here."

"We love it here," Mr. Terupt said, "but we want to be closer to Sara's family. We want Hope and our next baby and any babies after that to be close to Grandma and Grandpa and aunts and uncles."

This was all about family—a mother's love and looking out for her children. Suzie had shown me there was no stopping that.

"Family is most important," Jessica whispered, and sniffled.

"It is," Mr. Terupt agreed. "It's what brought your father here. He dropped everything for the chance to get back what he lost."

"And now you're dropping us," Peter added, his voice cold.

"Don't say it like that," Mr. Terupt said. "If I could have it both ways, you know I would. This is the way life plays out sometimes. You've got to find a way to make the most of it."

Make the most of it, I thought. "I have a way," I blurted. It had hit me out of nowhere, the way these things did sometimes. "It's an idea for our final project."

"A project?" Peter exploded. "Like that's going to make everything better. For such a brainiac, you can be really stupid sometimes." He grabbed his stuff and barged out the door. None of us tried to stop him, not even Mr. Terupt. Was this the beginning of the gang falling apart?

Mr. Terupt frowned. "It's understandable if you're upset with me, but please don't take it out on each other. In the end, it's one another you'll have to lean on."

That was Jeffrey's cue. He was the next to grab his things.

"Go check on him," Mr. Terupt said.

Jeffrey gave a slight nod and we watched him go.

"Luke, let's hear about your idea," Mr. Terupt said, returning his attention to the rest of us.

I glanced at the girls, who appeared ready to listen. I swallowed and then started explaining.

IF it was a good project,
THEN maybe there would be hope for the gang yet.

Jeffrey

I went to advising hoping Terupt would say something to Peter to fix him. At this point, I'd been to three varsity practices and Peter had gone to none. He'd skipped all of them. He hadn't put on his wrestling shoes since the day Terupt told us we were moving up. Coach Jennings had asked me where Peter was, and I'd covered for him, pretending he was sick. But that wasn't going to work forever. Terupt needed to confront Peter. That was all there was to it. He needed to say something to get Peter's head screwed on right again. Terupt fixed stuff like that.

But when advising came, no fixing happened. Peter blew up when Luke mentioned another project, and then he grabbed his stuff and barged out the door. Terupt never even tried to stop him.

"It's understandable if you're upset with me, but please don't take it out on each other," he said. "In the end, it's one another you'll have to lean on."

I glanced at Anna. *We* were the problem I needed to fix, but I didn't know how. I couldn't . . . because I had excuses. Lots of them. And because I was too chicken. But Peter was a different story. I pushed back my chair and grabbed my things.

"Go check on him," Terupt said.

I hurried out the door and spotted Peter already halfway down the hall. He had his earbuds in and wasn't looking back. I ran to catch up and shoved his shoulder.

He stumbled, then spun around and faced me. "What's your problem?" he snarled, yanking out his earbuds.

"What's *your* problem?" I responded.

"Don't you get it? He's done with us," Peter said, gesturing back down the hall. "He doesn't care—and neither do I."

"About anything?" I pressed. "You don't care about anything?"

He didn't answer, which was all the answer I needed. The truth was Terupt cared—and so did Peter, but he was hurting.

"Are you gonna quit and give up on everything just because the guy is moving?"

"Shut up!" he snapped. He tried walking away again, but I grabbed him.

"Get your hands off me," he spit, shaking free from my grasp.

"Peter, I've been down the road you're on," I said, my voice rising. "After my brother Michael died, I quit and didn't care about anything. And you know what? It didn't make anything better. It only made things worse."

His scowl deepened and his chin dropped, but he made no move to leave. I kept going.

"You can stay mad at Terupt all you want, but you can't quit on everything else," I said. "You can't bag wrestling. We're on this journey together, and we're just getting started. The varsity practices are good. They're tough. But I need you with me. Iron sharpens iron, remember?"

He looked at me.

"Don't throw it all away, Peter. If you do, the only person you're going to be mad at in the end is you."

We stood staring at each other, but neither one of us said anything more. Then Peter stuck his earbuds back in and walked away—and this time I let him go. Only time would tell if my words had gotten through to him.

ANNA

Peter stormed out of advising before we were finished and Jeffrey wasn't far behind, chasing after his buddy. He was worried about Peter, but not about me. Do I sound bitter? I was. But Jeffrey leaving was for the better anyway. I wasn't feeling comfortable being that close to him. Maybe he was feeling the same way, or maybe he was done with all feelings for me. Things with Danielle and me weren't much better. We were back to small talk but that was about it. But it wasn't nearly as suffocating around her as it was with Jeffrey—though I was dying to tell her the news about Mom because I was the only one who knew so far.

"Luke, let's hear about your idea," Mr. Terupt said.

Luke glanced at us. We nodded, letting him know it was okay, and he began.

"Well, my farm project is due soon, so I've been thinking about what could be next, and I think I've found it. The same way people sometimes have a bucket list of things they want to experience before passing on, I was thinking each of us could come up with a bucket-list item to share with Mr. Terupt before he moves on." He shrugged. "That's it. Kind of simple, but at the same time, big."

I didn't know how to respond. Bucket-list items were generally things like jumping out of planes or hot-air balloon rides. I wasn't sure I was up for that craziness, but apparently Mr. Terupt was.

"I like it," he said. "Saying goodbye is going to be just as tough for me as it will be for all of you. If we do this right, I think it will help."

"But what is right?" Lexie asked. "I mean, like, what sorts of things are we supposed to do?"

Luke shrugged again. "I haven't gotten that far yet."

"It can be anything," Jessica decided, "and it doesn't need to be over-the-top, like skydiving or bungee jumping. It only needs to be important."

The bell rang and Luke jumped to his feet. "I've got to go. I have a biology review session." He grabbed his backpack and scrambled toward the door.

"Bye, Luke," we called after him.

"Bye," he replied, giving us a glance on his way out.

Danielle smiled and waved to him. I wondered if she could breathe easier now that he was gone.

"Girls, I know you hate me, but would you be willing

and able to babysit again? Sara has a doctor appointment after school next week and I'll be tied up with practice. Any chance you could watch Hope for just a couple hours?"

"We don't hate you," Jessica said.

"Maybe just a little," Lexie corrected.

Jessica and I both elbowed her.

"We'd be happy to watch Hope," Jessica said, speaking for all of us.

"I mean, seriously, Teach, why would any of us say no?" Lexie added. "It's not like we're watching you. We're watching Hope, and we still love her."

We elbowed her again, but that didn't stop her.

"Besides," she continued, "it'll actually be the Babysitters Club this time, and not a gang. Mrs. Teach will like that."

That made us giggle. It was short-lived, but it felt good.

It was only a few days later when the Babysitters Club got together, excited to watch Hope. After Mrs. Terupt went over things and left for her appointment, we stayed in the family room. Jessica and I were having fun reading to Hope. She loved it when we read *Polar Bear, Polar Bear, What Do You Hear?* and made noises for the different animals.

"You two sound ridiculous," Lexie groaned from the couch, where she sat flipping through the TV channels.

"Let's hear you do better," Jessica challenged.

To our surprise, Lexie accepted. She handed me the remote and picked up the book. Her elephant was good, but her gorilla dance had us cracking up. The best part was the crazy look Hope flashed Lexie. We were dying from laughter when Danielle came out of the bathroom and went straight for her bag. We were obnoxiously loud, but Danielle didn't even bother looking at us. I watched her sit down and take out a bunch of her diabetes stuff.

"What're you doing?" Lexie asked.

"My pump site ripped off when I pulled my pants down, so now I need to replace it."

"You've got everything you need?" Jessica asked.

"Yes," Danielle answered. If it's possible to roll your eyes with your voice, Danielle had just done it.

"You're sure?" Jessica continued, missing the cues.

"Yes," Danielle snapped. "And I don't need any more mothers, so stop pestering me."

I'd seen Danielle get annoyed with her own mother for asking countless questions like those, but Jessica and Lexie were startled. It was supposed to be Lexie who knew how to put someone in their place, not Danielle. But Danielle had done just that, and Jessica and Lexie didn't dare say anything more. I had to bite the insides of my cheeks to keep from laughing.

We watched Danielle do her thing. There was so much to her pump. So much to having diabetes. And she never complained. She just dealt with it 24/7. When you stopped to think about that, it was both impressive and unfair. But she had everything under control—until she didn't.

"Sh—" Danielle cussed. It was under her breath, but we still heard it. Boy, did we take notice then. "I can't believe this," she moaned.

"What's wrong?" Jessica asked. She was playing with fire.

"My stupid backup site just broke," Danielle explained. "There must've been something wrong with it. The problem is I don't have another one with me."

"I do," I said. I got up from the floor and walked over to where I had my bag in the corner. I reached inside and pulled out a whole new set of Danielle's supplies. "And I'm not being another mother," I said, handing her the stuff. "I'm being your best-friend-slash-sister, and I'm sorry."

"You carry my supplies with you?" Danielle croaked.

"Ever since the wedding," I confessed. "That really scared me."

Danielle stood up and we hugged. "Thank you," she whispered, "and I'm sorry for not being there when you needed me."

We squeezed each other tight. "My mom's pregnant," I said. I couldn't keep it to myself any longer.

Danielle gasped.

"It's been so hard not telling you."

We hugged and danced. "We're such a messed-up family," Danielle said, and giggled. "You're going to be a sister, I'm going to be the aunt, and my mom will be the grandma."

More hugging and dancing. Hope joined in the giggling now.

"Okay. Like what in the heck is going on?" Lexie asked. "Were you guys fighting or something? And there's a baby on the way?"

"Nothing is going on," I said. "Everything is okay now.

And yes, my mom is pregnant, but don't tell. Nobody knows yet."

"Anna, that's wonderful," Jessica said.

When Mom first told me, my thought was, Great, I've gone from little attention to no attention. A pang of guilt passed through me for thinking that, but those feelings faded. Things were better with Mom and me now—and they were better with Danielle too. There was going to be a baby!

I smiled and then Danielle sat down with her supplies.

"Oh my goodness, I have an idea for the bucket list," Jessica announced.

"What!" Lexie shrieked. "These two just got done having a makeout session and you get an idea for the bucket list. Like, what the heck?"

"Actually, I've been thinking about what we could do ever since Luke's announcement at advising, and now I've got it. The bucket list should be about celebrating Mr. Terupt and each other and all that he's taught us—in memorable ways. It needs to be us working together to pull off something big and adventurous."

"Blah blah," Lexie said. "Cut to the chase. What's your idea?"

Jessica glanced at Danielle and her pump supplies. Then she patted the polar bear on the cover of Hope's board book. "Let's put on a Polar Plunge to raise money and awareness for diabetes."

I liked her idea immediately.

Danielle

Anna loved Jessica's Polar Plunge idea, but I wasn't so sure.

"I don't know. I don't want to make it all about me," I said.

"It won't be all about you," Jessica explained. "It's bigger than us, which is something Mr. Terupt has taught us to see."

"You're not the only one with diabetes, you know," Anna said.

I shrugged. "You really think people will pay money to jump in freezing water?"

"Absolutely" Jessica said. "The craziness of it will attract teenagers and the good-cause piece will get others involved."

Anna and Jessica were really excited, but Lexie hadn't said anything.

"Lex, are you okay?" Jessica asked, also noticing how quiet Lexie was.

"Yeah, I'm fine," Lexie said. "The Polar Plunge is a great idea. But like, who's supposed to do it?"

"Haven't you been listening?" Jessica asked. "Students. Teachers. Us," she said.

"Oh, no. There's no way I'm jumping in that water!" Lexie objected. She wasn't quiet anymore—and neither was Hope. Lexie's outburst had startled her and she began crying.

Anna picked her up and consoled her.

"To qualify as a bucket-list event, the gang must participate. That is an unwritten rule," Jessica maintained.

"Well, so sorry," Lexie said. "Not a chance."

Jessica peeked at me and winked. She was going to let Lexie have her drama-queen moment, knowing Lexie would change her mind eventually. I laughed and then I got started changing my pump site.

We spent the rest of Babysitters Club talking over ideas and details for our Polar Plunge. It was going to be a tremendous amount of work to pull off, but my friends were determined, and when had we ever backed down from a challenge?

When Mrs. Terupt returned from her appointment, we shared our idea with her and she thought it was great. She assured us Mr. Terupt would be thrilled.

"If I'm supposed to do it, he needs to do it too," Lexie insisted.

"I'll be sure to tell him," Mrs. Terupt said, and smirked.

We did our usual thank-yous and goodbyes and then we left. Mom was the one picking us up that afternoon. We gave Lexie and Jessica a ride to Lexie's house, but Anna came home with us. We got out of the car and hurried into the house ahead of Mom so we could slip past Grandma and sneak up to my room.

We plopped on my bed, giddy and excited just to be done fighting. "Wait until we tell Luke about the Polar Plunge. He's going to be so excited," I said, and giggled.

"You like him, don't you?" Anna said.

"No," I scoffed, trying to hide the truth.

"Danielle, stop pretending. I know you like him."

"I can't help it," I confessed, and sighed. "I didn't mean for it to happen. We've just been together so much, working on his project."

"I know."

"Do you think Jessica will be mad at me?" I worried.

"No."

"Really?"

"Actually, I don't know," Anna admitted. "Does she even like Luke like that anymore? Does he like her like that?"

I shrugged. "Maybe you can find out," I suggested.

Anna shook her head. "No. I don't want to get in the middle."

"You won't be in the middle," I said. "Nothing has happened. You're just doing some digging. Please."

She didn't say anything.

"Please," I said again.

"Okay, but only because I think he likes you."

"Thank you," I said, and hugged her. "I've never felt like this before."

"Well, be careful," Anna warned. "You don't want to get dumped like me."

"Anna, I'm sorry. I should've been there for you. I should've known. I wasn't a good sister or friend."

She shrugged. "You tried and I didn't let you. It's okay."

"It's not," I countered. "I'm going to find out what's going on with him."

"No," she insisted.

"Yes," I said. "You do some digging and I'll do some digging. A fair exchange. It's time for the Spy Sisters again."

Anna didn't get to object a second time because there was a knock on my door and Grandma waltzed in. "Dinner will be ready in twenty minutes," she said.

"How'd you know we were up here?" I asked.

"Oh, let's just say I remember sneaking off to my bedroom and gossiping with my girlfriend. Talking about school and clothes and such."

"School and clothes?" Anna asked.

"That's right," Grandma said. "And such." She winked and left just as quickly as she'd appeared.

"We better pray," I said. "She's on to us."

We held hands and bowed our heads.

"Dear God, it's us, Danielle and Anna. We have a few favors to ask. One: Please help me to make things right again for Anna and Jeffrey. Two: Please help me to do the right thing with Luke and Jessica—I don't want to make a mess of things. And three—very important: Please help me with Grandma. If she tries to get involved in my love life I don't know what'll happen."

Anna couldn't keep from giggling when I said that, but it was true.

"And lastly, more than anything, we pray for Baby Terupt Number Two and for Charlie and Terri and their baby on board."

We squeezed hands.

"Amen."

Alexia

Jess sensed there was something bothering me, but she also knew I didn't want to talk about it at Teach's house, so like, she waited until we were alone, but not a minute longer. We walked into my bedroom and she planted her tush in my chair and was like, "Okay, Lex, so what's wrong?"

I shrugged.

"Lex, it's me. You don't need to hold back. Spit it out."

I picked up Margo and sat on my bed. I cuddled her tight and then I took a deep breath and started talking.

"You know how Danielle has her diabetes to deal with every day?"

Jessica nodded.

"Well, this cancer stuff is sort of like that for me. I know it's not the same, because, like, I don't have to deal with it

225

the same way, but it's always there, in the back of my mind. Will Mom stay in remission? What if my results . . . Forget it. I sound stupid."

"No, you don't," Jessica said. "Your feelings are real; they're not stupid."

"There's more," I said. "When you started talking about a Polar Plunge to raise money for diabetes I kinda got angry. I wish I'd thought of doing something like that for breast cancer."

"Lexie, that's a great idea," Jessica exclaimed. "You definitely shouldn't feel bad about wanting that. We can make breast cancer the focus of our second bucket-list event."

"Yeah, maybe," I said. "Anyways, once the cancer thing popped into my head I started thinking about you-know-what, and that was why I got all quiet."

"Do you want to open your results?" Jess asked.

"No!" I shouted, freaking out and scaring Margo so bad that my little pooch jumped down and hid under my bed.

"Okay, okay," Jess said. "I was just asking. How about we brainstorm ideas for a breast-cancer event instead?"

I nodded, but then I couldn't help it. I started crying. Quiet at first, but once Jessica noticed, forget it. It all came out.

"Lexie!" Jessica shrieked. She rushed to my side and wrapped me in a hug. I cried harder. "What's wrong?"

"I don't know," I hiccupped.

"Is it the results?"

I shrugged. "I'm scared."

"You know what I'm going to say: you need to talk to your mom."

Jessica held me until I had myself under control and was breathing semi-normal again, and then she leaned back and wiped my face with her sleeve. "Man, you are the poster child for emotional teenage girl," she said.

I grabbed a tissue from my nightstand and blew my nose. "It's only 'cause I've got my period."

"Pfft. Whatever," she scoffed, borrowing one of my favorite expressions.

We laughed. Margo came out from hiding and hopped back onto my lap. She licked my salty cheeks and I started feeling better.

"So, I think I have an idea for your breast-cancer event," Jessica said.

"Already?"

"Yes. I've read about these things before, but I'm warning you, it's very bold."

"Okay. What is it?"

"It would involve shaving heads," she said.

Jessica

Twenty questions . . .
was the game Dad and I played
every time we got in the car
to go someplace
when I was little.

"Remember twenty questions?" he asks
after picking me up from Lexie's.

I nod.

"Only yes or no questions," he reminds me.

Another nod.

"Okay. I'll start.
Does your animal have a heart?"

I scowl.

"Does it?" he repeats.

Yes, I answer.

"Does your animal's heart
help friends
who are struggling
with a departing teacher?"

I swallow,

because now I see
where this game
is going.
"Does your animal's heart
worry about
protecting her mom?"

Back to nodding.

"Your animal is grappling with what to do
because of the conflict
between her heart and her mind?"

Yes.

"With what to believe,
what to say,
and who to trust?"

Yes.

"Would your animal like to know
what's happening with her parents?"

Yes.

Dad pulls into the driveway
and parks.
"Mom still needs time,

but like me,
she's hoping my daughter
will let me back into her life."

That wasn't a question,
but I answer anyway.
Yes, I croak.

We lean across the middle
and hug.
"I love you," he whispers.

I love you too.

I remember
leaving Dad to find Mr. Terupt.
And now Mr. Terupt is leaving,
and I have found my dad again.

Peter

"Must be I give a good pep talk," Jeffrey said when he saw me coming into practice the next day.

"Must be," I said.

He pulled me into a bro hug. "It's me and you now. You ready?"

"Yeah, let's do this."

We changed into our gear and went out to the mats, where the team gathered before the start of every practice.

"Jacobs! Nice of you to make it," Coach Jennings teased. "I hope you're ready, because you won't find your mommy here."

The older guys snickered. I couldn't tell if Coach Jennings was serious or joking, but after staring me down he smirked, and then I knew he was only giving me a hard time.

I liked him immediately—but I didn't like that he made Jeffrey and me wait.

It was two weeks before we got to wrestle off for our spots. Coach Jennings wanted us to get comfortable with the guys on the team and used to the varsity practices first. The practices were longer and more intense, but Jeffrey and I were ready for all of it—and we were ready when we finally got to wrestle off.

I was all kinds of nervous, partly because I'd never had a wrestle-off before, but mostly because this was my first match ever without T in my corner. Thinking of him just got me angry—and that was good before a match. My anger kept my nerves from getting in the way and holding me back.

My competition was a sophomore named Kris. He wasn't very good, but he already had a varsity season under his belt, so he was more experienced than me. I was determined to win to show T that I didn't need him anymore.

After a quick first-period takedown, I rolled Kris over in a cross-face cradle and pinned him. Jeffrey took care of his opponent in the same fashion, making it official. We were the new 113- and 120-pound varsity starters.

"You know," Jeffrey said when we were waiting for our rides after practice, "that was our first match without Terupt in our corners."

"Yeah, I know. And we won, which just proves we don't need him anymore."

"We're gonna have to wrestle without him," Jeffrey acknowledged, "but that doesn't mean we don't need him anymore or that he still can't be a part of this."

"It does for me," I growled. "I don't get why you and everyone else have to keep bringing him up and pretending everything is going to be okay and that nothing has changed. It's never going to be the same again."

I slammed the doors open and walked outside. It was a bitter-cold night, but the last thing I wanted was to hear Jeffrey's excuses. Fortunately, Mom pulled into the parking lot shortly after that, so I wasn't stuck freezing for long.

"Well, how'd the wrestle-off go?" she asked the second I was inside the car.

"I won."

"Honey, that's great!" she exclaimed.

It was, but I wasn't feeling it—and I definitely wasn't feeling it after Jeffrey and I got thrown in with the big boys. We'd won our wrestle-offs and walked around feeling pretty special for a few days, but when we took to the mats at our first varsity tournament we got a taste of something we'd never experienced on the junior high team—defeat.

We got our butts kicked! I lost by eight and Jeffrey lost by six. We managed to squeak out wins in our consolation matches, but then we lost our next ones and were eliminated. Yes, we were only in eighth grade, and the guys we lost to were juniors and seniors in high school, but that didn't make it any easier.

Our parents tried to tell us we'd done a good job, but they just didn't get it. The one guy who always knew what to say wasn't around—and this was all his fault.

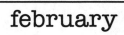
february

LUKE

**IF you share a great project idea,
THEN other people will get excited about it too—and
nothing brings people together like a great project.**

That was the truth. I'd seen it happen with us before. But so too was this statement:

**IF there is any hidden tension within a group,
THEN working together on a project will bring it
to the surface.**

As soon as the girls told me about a possible Polar Plunge for our first bucket-list event, I sat down and made a list of all the items I thought we'd need to make it a success. It was a brilliant idea on so many levels. This was the exact sort of thing I had in mind when I first proposed a bucket list. I envisioned big challenges—and this fit the bill. It was a huge undertaking. My farm project had been a terrific personal learning experience for which I earned an A-plus, but this Polar Plunge had the potential to be so much more. Not only were we doing it for a great cause—diabetes awareness—but it was for Danielle. After all the help she'd given me, I owed her.

"Okay, first things first," I said, turning our lunchtime into a business meeting. "We have to tell Mr. Terupt what we're planning, because we need to make advising time project time. That's the one period when we're all together, so we must take advantage of it. But I also want to make it clear that this endeavor is not supposed to be something that creates more work for Mr. Terupt. That's not what the bucket list is for. The bucket list is a way of celebrating what Mr. Terupt has taught us and our time with him."

"Save your load of crap for someone else," Peter growled.

"Peter!" Jessica gasped.

"What?" he responded. "Stop talking like the guy is a hero. He's a fake. He gives us these noble speeches and then takes the easy way out."

"Peter, stop," Lexie said.

"Peter nothing," he snapped, rising to his feet. "You know I'm right. The truth hurts." He grabbed his lunch tray and walked off.

"Let him go," Jeffrey said. "He'll come around eventually."

"I hope so," I said, "because none of this feels right if we don't have everyone on board."

Peter

I got so freaking angry when Luke started talking about celebrating T that I had to get out of there before I hauled off and punched him in the mouth. I tossed my lunch in the trash and headed straight to the office. I couldn't take it anymore. Something had to change.

I walked through the door and Mrs. Francine's cheeks turned beet red when she glanced up and saw me.

"Mrs. Francine, can you please let Principal Lee know that I'm here and need to see him? It's urgent."

Mrs. Francine nodded and scurried away. A minute later she returned. "Mr. Lee said you can go in," she said, averting her eyes from mine. "And don't worry, I won't be interrupting."

I snickered at her remark, but all amusement was gone by the time I stepped into Mr. Lee's office.

"Mr. Jacobs, what seems to be the urgent matter?"

"I need to be moved out of Mr. Terupt's advising group. You can put me anyplace else."

Mr. Lee's eyes narrowed. He sat forward, placing his forearms on his desk. "Mr. Jacobs—"

"I don't want to talk about it. Please just make the switch for me."

Mr. Lee leaned back in his chair and sighed. Then he turned and pulled a movie from his shelf. "I'm not putting you in a different group, but I'll grant you permission to go to the library during advising, provided you agree to watch this movie."

"Deal," I said. Getting out of T's advising was worth any extra assignment—and this one was easy.

"When your emotions have calmed down, you can come back and we'll talk."

I didn't respond. I took his movie and left. Mission accomplished.

Jeffrey

Terupt took me aside during advising, which was now project time. He knew my move to varsity hadn't been an easy one, and this was the first chance he'd had to talk to me. There were always other kids around in between classes, and never enough time. "Keep your head up and keep working hard—it will get better," he'd told me, but he hadn't been able to say much more than that. And that was the same stuff my parents and Coach Jennings were already telling me. I needed more than that—and he knew it. So did Peter, but he wasn't there. He'd gone to Principal Lee and got permission not to come to our advising group so he wouldn't have to be anywhere near Terupt. It was bad.

"Heard you had a tough weekend," Terupt said, taking a seat beside me.

"I've had a few tough weekends," I said, staring at the floor. Peter and I had competed in two tournaments and two away dual meets at this point, and the results weren't very good. We'd done more losing than winning.

"Coach Jennings says you and Peter are doing terrific."

"I don't call losing terrific."

Terupt snorted. "Me neither. But at least you've gotten it out of the way. Now you don't have to worry about it anymore."

I gave him a funny look. What was he talking about?

"Think about it," he continued. "What's the worst that can happen? You lose? That's already happened, so stop being scared of it."

I shrugged.

"Jeffrey, if you're scared of losing, you hold back, you don't do your best. Don't even think about winning and losing. Instead, focus all of your energy on simply competing as hard as you can from start to finish, and then good things will happen."

I guessed that made sense. I could do that.

"Some of history's very best wrestlers lost their first outings. But once they got over the mental challenge, they went on to greatness. Perhaps the most important thing here is that you don't like losing. In fact, you hate it. And that is why you're going to work even harder to get better. Am I right?"

I nodded. "Yes," I said, feeling more determined already.

He patted me on the shoulder. "Remember, it's not where you start, it's where you finish."

"Thanks."

"I'll be there for your home match next week. I can't wait to see you and Peter in varsity singlets."

"He'll come around eventually," I told Terupt, same as I'd told the gang.

"I hope so."

He got up and left. A few seconds later Danielle slipped into the chair where he'd been sitting. Terupt had given me a pep talk. Danielle had something else in store.

Danielle

I always looked forward to advising because it was the one time when we had the gang and Mr. Terupt together, though the "gang" part of things wasn't exactly perfect. For one thing, Peter wasn't with us. He wanted nothing to do with Mr. Terupt. And I worried he might not be our only problem. If I didn't get myself under control, would things with Luke and Jessica get ugly? Was there still something there? And there was the ongoing issue between Jeffrey and Anna.

One step at a time, I reminded myself. That approach always worked well on the farm. First up, some digging with Jeffrey. I'd told Anna I was going to do it, and advising was my best opportunity. Before I could get to that, though, Luke had plans of his own.

He took charge from the start, assigning us different

jobs that needed to be done to make our Polar Plunge successful. I was responsible for creating posters to advertise the event. Jessica and Lexie were doing their part on social media to drum up support, while Anna was looking into what we had to do to make this an official event for the Juvenile Diabetes Research Foundation. Jeffrey was busy doing something else.

Luke was right to call this a project. It was a project with a capital *P*. There was so much to do. With his father's help, Luke had already secured a date and spot for our plunge. He scheduled it for the last Sunday in February, down on the Long Island Sound, in the same area where the summer festival had occurred.

"My dad and I thought that would be a good spot because the pier is there. We can have participants jump off the end and swim to shore."

My expression didn't hide my surprise. Suddenly, this had gone from a mere idea to a real thing.

"We've got two lifeguards coming, and we're going to have a medical tent too," Luke continued.

Now my eyes were wide. "Luke, you've done all this already?" I said.

He shrugged. "It's our first bucket-list event, and it's for a great cause."

I smiled.

"And it's for you," he mumbled.

My cheeks burned. I cast a nervous glance in Jessica's direction, but her face was hidden behind a computer screen.

Had she heard him? I didn't know, but there wasn't anything I could do except get to work.

I found Mr. Terupt's construction paper and markers. I had planned to sit near Jeffrey, but Mr. Terupt beat me to it. I was afraid I'd missed my chance for digging, but luckily, Mr. Terupt didn't spend that long chatting. When he moved along, I waited a few seconds and then I slid in beside Jeffrey. It was my turn.

When it came to digging, I only knew how to do it one way: you sank your shovel in as far as you could and pried.

"Why did you break up with Anna?" I said. Just came right out and asked him. Sank my shovel all the way in.

His head whipped in my direction. Clearly, he hadn't expected that. His mouth opened and closed.

I sank my shovel deeper. "Why'd you do it?" I pressed.

His shoulders sagged. "I don't know. I mean, I do, but it was dumb. I wish I could take it back."

I hadn't been sure how he'd answer, but this was good news. "So why haven't you tried fixing it?"

"I don't know how," he confessed. "And I don't know if she wants me to. Or if she'll ever forgive me."

"You can't be afraid of losing," I said.

Jeffrey eyed me suspiciously. Yes, I'd heard a little of what Mr. Terupt had said. It was good advice. He always gave good advice.

"Why don't you bring Asher to the farm so he can see our newest calf, and so you can talk to Anna," I suggested.

Jeffrey shrugged. "Okay, but when? I've got wrestling after school and on Saturdays."

"It'll have to be Sunday afternoon, then. Anna will be with me because we always have Sunday dinner together, so make it around two o'clock."

"Do you think she'll forgive me?" Jeffrey asked.

"Not if you don't ask," I said, sounding a bit like Mr. Terupt.

ANNA

I couldn't stay inside the house any longer. Danielle told me Jeffrey would be coming by with Asher and I was too nervous to sit still. I was up and down more than Mom with her morning sickness. I went into the barn to visit with the mama cows, hoping their comfort would help settle me down.

Danielle agreed to play lookout. She was going to let me know when Jeffrey and Asher arrived, but for the time being, it was just me and the cows, a barn cat or two, and some soft country music. I grabbed a broom to keep busy. I swept the area in front of the stalls, pushing the loose hay together so the cows could eat it. I was near the end of the row when Danielle called, "They're here."

My legs turned weak and my heart thumped inside my

chest. I reminded myself of an old fixer-upper car, one that could break down any second. But then Asher came plodding into the barn and I couldn't help but smile.

"Anna!" he squealed when he saw me, breaking into a run. I kneeled down and met him with a big hug.

"Hi, Asher," I whispered. "I've missed you."

"Cows eat," he said, pointing at the mamas. "They's hungry."

I giggled. "Yes, they're hungry. You can feed them if you want." I picked up a piece of straw and showed Asher how to hold it for the cow to grab. He squealed to high heaven when he saw that. I swear, even the cows' eyes grew bigger at the sound. Asher took a piece of hay and held it out for the nearest cow and she began pulling at it with her tongue. He clapped after she'd eaten it, and then he bent down and found another piece to hold. I smiled and stood up.

"Hey," Jeffrey whispered.

We made eye contact but then quickly looked away. I stared at the hay while Jeffrey scuffed his foot on the ground. I waited to see if he had anything more to say.

"Anna . . . I'm sorry," he finally managed.

I didn't respond. His apology was enough—and it wasn't. I still had a lot of questions. Did he mean it? And how could I trust that he meant it? Why did he do it? And so much more.

"Anna, I'm . . . I . . ." He stopped and started, searching for the right words, but all he could find was "I'm sorry."

I nodded.

"I was hoping you'd come to my match Wednesday night. It'll be my first time wrestling varsity at home, but it's the team's last home meet of the season."

"Why?" I asked, looking at him now. "Why do you want me there? I thought I was a distraction."

He shook his head. "When I glance into the stands and you aren't there, that's when I can't focus."

"So you want me there so you'll feel better and can concentrate on your match?"

He nodded.

"It's all about you and winning, isn't it?" I began walking away.

"No. Anna, wait. Please."

I stopped.

"I didn't mean it like that," he sputtered.

I spun around. "So how do you mean it?" I pushed.

"Everything I said to you when . . . I didn't mean any of it. My head was messed up and I was searching for excuses. I blamed you when none of it was your fault. I know I hurt you and I'm sorry. I just want things to go back to the way they were—but I'm scared you might not want that."

He'd finally said something true and from his heart. He'd said what I was so hoping to hear. But you know what? I also heard Lexie's voice telling me not to let him off easy after what he did. So I made him stand there, waiting for me to say something. And then all I gave him was "I'll think about it."

"C'mon, Asher," I said, turning to my little buddy. "Let's go see the new baby."

Asher took my hand and off we went. I walked with my chin up and my shoulders back. I'd probably go to Jeffrey's match, but he could sweat about that a little more. Lexie was rubbing off on me—and that wasn't always such a bad thing.

Peter

I peeked into the gym. The stands were filling up for our dual against Xavier. It may have been our last home meet of the season, but it was my and Jeffrey's first-ever varsity match in front of the home crowd. The two of us stayed out of sight, hidden in the wrestling room. We turned our attention to the mat and focused on getting a good drill to warm up, hoping that would help to calm our nerves.

Jeffrey told me he was only thinking about wrestling hard from start to finish and the heck with winning or losing, and I thought that was a smart approach until he told me where he got that advice. Hearing more about Coach T just made me angry, but like I said earlier, being angry was good before my match.

Coach Jennings gathered the team when it was time to

get the show going. He gave us his pre-match pep talk and then we lined up with the senior captains in the front. The gym went black except for the sole spotlight hanging above our mat. AC/DC began blasting through speakers and we jogged out. The crowd went nuts, hooting and cheering. Goose bumps covered my body. It was awesome.

When our warm-up song ended we stood along the edge of the mat and did some quick honoring-seniors stuff, since this was the last time any of them would wrestle at home, and then it was on to team introductions. I glanced into the bleachers during the national anthem and spotted the gang. Jeffrey noticed them too. I hoped Anna being there was a good thing. Sitting in front was Coach T. Maybe he gave solid wrestling advice, but there was nothing he could say or do to make his ditching us and running away any better. Anger sizzled inside me.

When the national anthem was over, it was finally time to wrestle. There was a forfeit in the 106-pound weight class because Xavier didn't have a wrestler, so I was the first match of the night. I liked that because it gave me less time to be nervous. I was ready to show T that I didn't need him.

"Let's go, Peter," the crowd cheered when I took the mat.

I shook hands with my opponent and the ref blew his whistle. And after that, it's all a blur. I don't remember any-thing about how I scored and he scored. I tend to remember the matches I lost way more than the ones I won—and I won that night. And so did Jeffrey. We wrestled hard from start to finish. The gym was crazy-loud after our strong start.

We'd set the team on fire, and we never slowed down. We steamrolled Xavier. It was a great night—but it wasn't over yet. I might not remember all the details of my match, but I sure remember what happened after the wrestling was done.

The gang came and found me and Jeffrey. "You guys were great!" Luke exclaimed. "You kicked their butts."

I grinned. It was funny to hear Luke talking tough like that. "Thanks, Lukester."

"Thanks for coming," Jeffrey said, his eyes locked on Anna. She nodded.

"Are you kidding! That was awesome!" Luke raved. "I'm definitely going to your next meet."

"Lukester, that was our last home match," I reminded him. "Our post-season tournaments start now."

"I don't care. I'm going," he said.

"Us too," Anna agreed, speaking for the girls. Boy, was Jeffrey smiling after she said that.

"That's right," Jessica echoed. "It's like we've always said, we do our best when we have everyone together."

Here it comes, I thought. They'd laid the trap. She and Lexie must've had this planned. Too bad. I wasn't doing their Polar Plunger and that was that. I wasn't doing anything that had anything to do with T. They knew how I felt and had left me alone throughout all of their preparations, but now that the date was around the corner, Lexie was out of patience. "Peter, you've got to do the plunge with us," she pleaded. "It won't be right if you don't. Please." She batted her eyes.

"I've gotta go," I said. "Thanks for coming." I grabbed

my headgear and sweatshirt from the bench—and then something stopped me. This is going to sound weird, but it was Beethoven. The familiar tune started playing out of nowhere.

"Ugh," Danielle groaned. "That's my pump. It plays Beethoven as a warning whenever I get low on insulin. Sorry."

I stood there, watching her push buttons on her device. Every day, I thought. Every day she has to deal with that. And I'd never heard her complain. Would I be able to wrestle if I had diabetes? I thought back to last year, when I was locked in the closet with her, and I felt the same urge to help her all over again.

"I'll do it," I said. "I'll be there for your Polar Plunger. But let's get one thing straight. I'm not doing it for T or any silly bucket-list thing. I'm doing it for you." I pointed at Danielle. "I want to help because I don't know how you deal with that crap every single day like you do."

"It's because she's amazing," Luke said.

Danielle's cheeks turned red, and I thought maybe it was because she needed to fix her pump and her sugars, but when I noticed Luke's face doing the same thing I realized it was something else. I glanced at Jessica, but she seemed unfazed. Maybe they weren't a thing anymore.

"Thanks, Peter," Lexie whispered, leaning in and kissing me on the cheek.

"I've gotta go now," I said. T was done chatting with Coach Jennings, and he was headed in our direction. Maybe I was ready for the Polar Plunger, but I wasn't ready for more than that.

Alexia

Jessica nudged me. We were just wrapping things up during our last project/advising session before the big Polar Plunge. It was time.

I cleared my throat. "So like, I think I have an idea for our next bucket-list event," I said. "I mean, for after we finish with the Polar Plunge."

Everyone stopped what they were doing and looked at me. I glanced at Jessica and she nodded, encouraging me to continue.

"Jess and I have been talking about it, but like, we haven't mentioned it because we didn't want to make it seem like I was competing with Danielle. It's not like that. But doing this thing for diabetes has, like, made me want to do something for breast cancer. You know, after everything that happened with my mom."

"Lexie, that's wonderful," Teach said, putting me at ease. Danielle and Anna smiled.

"What's the idea?" Luke asked, already excited.

"We were thinking we could host a head-shaving event," Jessica answered. "Perhaps the hair could go toward making wigs for patients, and the money we raise would be donated to breast cancer research."

"Wow! That would be another big event!" Luke cheered, but then he thought of something and his face scrunched. "Who's going to shave their head?" he asked, confused.

"I will," Teach replied.

The knot in my throat formed immediately. So did the tears in my eyes and the ache in my heart. I threw my arms around him and squeezed. I held him tight, but I was already missing him.

I was overcome with emotion because, like, this event was for breast cancer and people like my mom, but it was possible it was for me too—and that scared me. I still hadn't told Mom about the GeneLink test or opened my results—because that scared me more.

"I'll shave my head too," Jeffrey said.

I pulled back from Teach's chest and peeked at Jeffrey. He smiled. "I know about cancer too," he said, reminding us of Michael.

"Lexie and I have discussed this at length," Jessica continued, "and we agree, if we want to make this event what it has the potential to be, and if we want it to be a true bucket-list undertaking, then we all need to participate."

"When you say participate, do you mean, we should all shave our heads?" Luke asked.

Jess nodded. "Girls included."

My hands went to my head. My hair. What would bald feel like? I wondered.

"We challenge the school to raise X amount of dollars, and if they meet the challenge, then we get our heads shaved," Jessica continued.

"Whoa," Luke said. "Whoa."

"I'll do it," Anna said.

"Me too," Danielle agreed.

I glanced at Teach, and he was wiping his eyes. I got it. I understood.

Leaving advising that afternoon, Danielle and Anna pulled me aside. "Lexie, did you get your results?" they whispered so that no one else heard them.

I shook my head and they sighed. It was obvious they'd forgotten. Farm projects and boyfriend problems could do that to a person—just not me. As much as I would've liked to forget, I hadn't. I'd never forget.

Jeffrey

Before the Polar Plunge and before any head-shaving event, Peter and I still had wrestling to do. It was the post-season now. First up was our Division Tournament. This was a big one. The top five guys in each weight class moved on to the State Championships the following weekend. Those who didn't make the top five hung up their shoes and called it a season.

I wasn't ready to be finished, and neither was Peter, but we had our work cut out for us. I entered the tournament unseeded in my weight class and Peter was ranked twelfth in his. Bottom line: We both needed to beat kids who were supposed to be better than us if we wanted to keep going.

Coach Terupt was always good at the pep talks, but it

was Coach Jennings who knew what to tell me and Peter this time.

"Okay, boys, listen up. The seeds don't mean anything. If you guys had wrestled varsity all season you'd be seeded higher, plain and simple. All this means is you get to show up and surprise people today."

I smiled at that, and so did Peter. "Let's do this," he said. We high-fived and began warming up.

The day was full of the unexpected. Peter knocked off the number four seed in one of his early matches and then I went out and beat the number five seed in my weight. Was I surprised? Maybe a little.

I was more surprised when I spotted Coach Terupt and the gang sitting in the bleachers near my family. They'd made it.

"Thanks for coming," I said to them.

"Wouldn't miss it," Anna said, and smiled.

"I told you I was going to be here," Luke reminded me. "This is even more exciting than your last match."

We laughed at his enthusiasm.

"Keep letting it fly out there," Coach Terupt encouraged me. "Tell Peter the same."

I nodded.

"Fly Ree," Asher cheered. I rubbed my little brother's head.

The next round didn't go quite as well. Peter and I both lost to the top-seeded wrestlers in our weights, but we only lost by a few points. As eighth graders we went toe-to-toe with seniors, and while I hated losing, in a way, that was a small win for us. And our day wasn't over. After another pair of wins in the consolation rounds and a narrow loss, Peter and I found ourselves wrestling for fifth place. Win and go to States. Lose and sit home.

I checked in with Coach Terupt. "You and Peter have similar opponents. They're teammates and probably drill partners, so they wrestle alike. You need to close the distance and wrestle from a tie-up. They can only shoot from space. Stay on them and they won't have any attack."

"Got it," I said.

"Who drills harder every day at practice? You and Peter, or those guys?" Terupt asked.

That wasn't even a question. It was time to show him.

Peter

One day after Jeffrey and I shocked the world by placing fifth at the Divisions and qualifying for States, I stood in the parking lot of the Polar Plunger, surveying the scene. You know what they say, no rest for the wicked.

As I stood there, I suddenly realized I never really stopped to consider what I'd agreed to. This thing was happening in the same area where Lexie got zapped by that jellyfish, except this wasn't any summertime fun. It was so cold there were lifeguards dressed in hard-core wetsuits, ready to save me in case my body quit from being frozen, but I was supposed to jump in with just my swim trunks on. This was nuts! But wait—if I managed to survive the plunge and make the swim back to shore, there was a large tent set up on the beach, with blankets and heaters inside and people serving hot chocolate, so that made it all better. Ha!

Despite the single-digit temperatures, a lot of locals and kids from school still showed up. That made sense. The colder the crazier, and a teenager is always looking for some crazy way to have fun. And what better fun than watching your friends suffer in ice water?

Besides Danielle being an all-around awesome person and loved by teachers, the only possible explanation behind all the adults being there was that the gang had done a knockout job of advertising and getting things ready for today. Pulling this off must've been a ton of work, but I wasn't surprised. I pretended not to care, but it bothered me that I hadn't done anything. I promised myself I wouldn't let that happen again.

"Peter, you made it," Luke said when he spotted me staring out at the water.

"Yeah, I made it."

"It's cold, huh?" he said, shivering.

"No," I scoffed.

"Yes, it is," he argued, taking me seriously. "Based on my calculations, factoring into account the water temperature, wind, and average body size, a person will succumb to hypothermia in approximately three minutes in that water."

"Good thing we're getting in and getting out, then," I said.

"That's actually very important. That's why I volunteered us to go first, so everyone else sees how to do it."

"Us? Who's us?" I asked.

"The gang. Me and you," Luke responded.

I wanted to choke him. I figured I'd wait till the end,

see if I could weasel my way out of actually jumping, but not now.

"C'mon," he said. "Everyone else is inside the tent getting ready."

I followed him. They were getting ready, all right, if you call sipping hot chocolate getting ready. We hadn't even gone plunging yet.

"Hi, Peter," Anna said.

"Thanks for coming," Danielle said.

I gave her a fist bump.

We hung out for a bit and things were fine until you-know-who showed up. He had the missus and Hope with him. Hope was bundled head to toe. She had the right idea.

"Mrs. Terupt, will you be joining us?" Luke asked.

She shook her head. "I'm afraid not. I don't think that would be a good idea for baby on board," she said, patting her belly.

"Oh, yeah, right," Luke said. "I keep forgetting."

"If you felt like I do in the morning, you wouldn't be forgetting."

Mad at T or not, when she said that, I got worried. Was she okay? She must've seen the concern in our faces, because she quickly said, "Oh, don't worry. It was nothing more than routine morning sickness. I'm past it now. I'm just complaining."

"It's okay to complain, Mrs. Teach. No one likes throwing up," Lexie said.

Everyone nodded in agreement.

"Plunging will begin in five minutes," Luke's dad announced, sticking his head inside the tent.

Things got serious then . . . until we saw what Luke was wearing. I kicked off my sneakers and socks and got rid of my sweats, and when I straightened back up, there he was, standing before us—in a Speedo!

"Whoa, Lukester!" I crowed. "Looking sexy, buddy."

"Oh!" Lexie gasped, covering her eyes. "Luke, are you seriously wearing that?"

"Very seriously," he said. "I'm not going for sexy. I'm going for warmth, and these are going to work much better than everyday swim trunks."

"I'll deal with the cold," I said. "There's no way you'd catch me wearing those puppies."

"Keep talking," Luke said. "We'll see who's laughing in the end." He turned and strode out of the tent.

We shook our heads and followed him. I began shivering as soon as I stepped outside. The air was cold enough, and somehow I was supposed to get my body into that water. Nuts, I thought. Absolutely nuts.

"Plungers, line up!" Luke's father called through his megaphone.

I glanced behind me and saw T ready to go, and farther back I spotted Principal Lee, his hairy belly on full display. I wasn't sure if he or Luke looked worse, but it was cool of him to be there.

"Get set," Luke's dad boomed.

That was followed by a shrill blast from his whistle, and the plunging began. Our line marched down the pier. When you reached the end you jumped in and swam for your life to get back to the beach and out of that water as fast as possible. As bad as I've made it sound, it was worse.

Pinpricks covered my entire body. I couldn't feel my feet. Even my brain hurt. I was suffering from the world's worst ice cream brain freeze times ten. But it was my boys that hurt the most. They actually hurt. Luke was right. My trunks did nothing to protect them. They were immersed in the frigid waters, and now I feared they were frozen. Through it all, I somehow managed to reach the shore before drowning and sprinted across the sand and back inside the tent.

"Bet you wished you had my sexy Speedo now," Luke joked after we had our cocoas.

"Shut up," I growled.

The gang laughed, and then so did I. We stayed there, shivering and laughing together in that tent with our hot cocoas, and it felt good. Real good. That was the first I'd hung out with them and shared laughs like that since getting the news about T. Maybe that was what Luke was thinking when he came up with this bucket-list thing. I didn't know, but I liked it. I was still done with T, but I was gonna make sure I was involved in the rest of our bucket-list adventures—from start to finish.

"You think this one was bad. Just wait till you see what's in store for you next," Lexie said to me as we were leaving.

I stopped and looked at her. She kissed her fingers and

pressed them to my cheek. Then she turned and ran across the parking lot.

"What?" I yelled after her. "What is it?"

She never answered. I watched her climb into her car and disappear.

What could be worse?

Jessica

February . . .
was many things.
Cold, for one.
But my heart warmed
for Jeffrey and Peter
getting their hands raised
in a final dual meet and then again
at their Division Tournament.
Fifth-place finishes,
as mere eighth graders,
qualifying for the State Championship.
We couldn't wait to cheer them on again.

February
was many things.

Colder, for two.
But my heart warmed
for Lexie and her courage
to share her idea
for our next bucket-list event.
For Danielle after a successful Polar Plunge,
and for Luke
so proud of our success.

February
was many things.
Hard, for another.
My heart hurt
when I saw Peter still keeping Mr. Terupt away.
When I saw Mom slip her Valentine from Dad
back into its envelope,
tucked away with all his other words.
Fixing a broken heart was hard.

February
was many things.
The shortest month,
so maybe Cold
and Colder
and Hard
were behind us.
And March would be better.

March held the promise
of many things.

Haircuts, for one.
Perhaps opened results, for another.
Or State wrestling champions?
Maybe temperatures
would warm
and hearts would thaw
and repair?
March held possibility—and hope.

march

LUKE

IF you ignore your feelings,
THEN they will go away.

I was trying to prove this statement true—but it wasn't working. It was hard to forget when you were with a certain someone so often. Ignoring the situation was nearly impossible. I buried myself in schoolwork to keep from thinking about it too much, which was what I tried doing during Peter and Jeffrey's State Championships. Between their matches I camped out at the top of the bleachers with my computer and notebooks, but that didn't stop Anna. After those guys lost their second matches and were knocked out of the competition, she came and plopped down next to me.

"Luke, you're really good at science," she said. I thought

she'd said that because she saw all the notes and equations and diagrams for photosynthesis and cellular respiration that I was studying.

"Thanks," I replied.

"So I'm confused," she continued. "Have you really failed to notice the obvious, or are you pretending?"

Now I was confused. "What?"

"Luke, what's going on with you and Jessica?"

I hid behind my computer screen. "Nothing," I croaked.

"Okay. So what's going on with you and Danielle, then?"

Gulp. "Nothing," I croaked again—but Anna wasn't convinced.

"Hiding behind your computer screen doesn't make that true, you know. Hiding doesn't work. Trust me, I tried it for a long time."

I peeked and did a quick scan of the bleachers.

"Don't worry, it's just me. Everyone else went to the bathroom and to get something to eat. So, do you like her?"

"Danielle?" I asked.

"Yes, Danielle," she replied.

I nodded and Anna smiled. "But don't tell," I pleaded. "I don't want to hurt Jessica's feelings."

"So there is something going on with you and Jessica?" she asked.

"No. I don't think so. I don't know." I sighed. "I'm not good at this stuff."

"Don't worry," Anna said, patting my knee and standing. "I'll take care of Jessica."

"What're you going to do?" I asked.

"I'm going to talk to her."

"No," I protested. "You can't."

"I can. You're a wiz at school, but let me handle this. You just relax and go back to studying." She started down the bleachers.

Relax? Hardly. I would've bet my heart was racing faster than the wrestlers'. "Anna," I called before she got away. "Does Danielle . . ."

"Like you?" she finished for me.

I nodded.

Anna smiled and gave a small laugh. "Yes, but take it slow," she advised. "And it's probably best not to show it too much in front of Jessica until I've talked to her."

I responded with a thumbs-up. Anna turned and bounded down the rest of the bleachers and out of the gym. I sat still, but I felt like I was bounding too.

**IF you find out your feelings are mutual,
THEN they immediately grow stronger.**

Jeffrey

The Division Tournament had been a great day and the Polar Plunge a huge success, but our celebrating stopped there. Peter and I got to wrestle in the State Championships, which was a big accomplishment for eighth graders. Unfortunately, that was where our stories came to an end. We each won two matches, but we didn't place. Our seasons were over.

Mom and Dad gave me a hug and told me how proud they were, and you know what, it didn't make me mad this time.

"Ree lose," Asher said, explaining to me what had happened.

"Yeah, I lost, buddy."

"Ree all done?"

"Yup, I'm done now," I said, fighting the knot in my throat. Such simple questions, but painfully hard to answer. Losing was never easy.

My little brother was smart enough to see that. He wrapped his arms around me. I smiled and hugged him back. I could always count on Asher to make me feel better—him and Coach Terupt.

"Go get cookie," Asher said when we let go of each other. He showed me his half-eaten snickerdoodle.

"In a minute," I told him. I saw that Coach Terupt was headed toward me. He'd been chatting with Dad, and now it looked like it was my turn. "Let me talk to Coach Terupt first, and then we'll go, okay?"

"Otay," Asher agreed. He ran to tell Mom the exciting news.

"Bittersweet, isn't it?" Coach Terupt said, sitting beside me.

I nodded.

"Just think, the junior high season ended weeks ago. If you'd stayed with me, you would've missed all this."

I hadn't thought about that, but it was true. Moving up was hard, but it had definitely been the right thing to do.

"Jeffrey, it's important that you and Peter made it here this year. You got a taste of it, and now you know what to expect. You're going to win this someday—sooner rather than later. You and Peter. And when you do, I'll be here watching. That's a promise."

He patted me on the back and then he got up and

left. I still felt bad about losing, but I might've felt worse for Coach Terupt. Peter could go on shunning him all he wanted, but Terupt would never give up on him—or any of us. It took a special person to make me feel lucky even after losing.

anna

What I did with Luke wasn't digging, it was more like shining a flashlight. I had to point out the obvious for him. I would've done it sooner but I wanted to wait until no one else was around, and that didn't happen until Jeffrey and Peter were finished wrestling.

The talk with Luke was easy. Well, easy for me. Luke struggled, but he was happy in the end. After our chat I left him alone with his studies and feelings for Danielle and went to find Jessica. And to be clear, what I did with her wasn't digging, either. It was being a friend.

I found her sitting with Lexie at one of the tables out by the concessions. I didn't mind that Lexie was there. Call me crazy, but I actually thought she might be able to help smooth things over. After all, according to her,

Lexie was the queen of romance and relationships. But let's not forget, I had specialized in matchmaking for a long time.

"Okay if I join you?" I asked them.

"Of course," Jessica said. "Don't be silly."

I pulled out a chair and sat down. "Is Danielle in the bathroom?" I asked next, noticing that she wasn't in line.

"I think so," Jessica replied, fixing her pony.

"Do I stink?" Lexie demanded out of the blue, thrusting her arm under my nose.

I recoiled.

"Seriously, do I stink?" she repeated.

I leaned forward and carefully sniffed her shirt. "No."

"Phew," she sighed with relief. "Thank Danielle's God. Honestly, I don't know how you three can stand it. I couldn't even breathe in that gym, it stinks so bad."

Jessica rolled her eyes and I giggled.

"Whatever," Lexie snipped. "When you appreciate nice perfumes and fragrances you notice stuff like repulsive boy smells."

Jessica and I laughed harder. Then I took a breath and started digging. I had to before Danielle returned and it was too late—and before I lost the nerve. Being a friend isn't always easy.

"Jessica, I think Luke and Danielle have developed feelings for each other since doing all of these projects together," I said. "And I think they're afraid because they're worried about you."

"Are you serious?" Lexie freaked. "Those two like each other? How in the world did I miss that?"

"Shhh," I urged, trying to quiet her.

"Worried about me?" Jessica said. "I've been worried about *them*. I've noticed the way they've been acting and I've tried ignoring it, hoping it would blossom. I want them together."

"You do?!" I exclaimed. It was my turn to freak out.

"Shhh," Lexie hissed, giving me a taste of my own medicine.

"Yes," Jessica continued. "I just don't feel that way about Luke. Besides, it's not like we were ever a real couple. Yes, we shared a moment at the end of last year, but that was it. I'll admit there was a spark, but we didn't see enough of each other to keep that flame going. It was juvenile love, not the real thing. We're better off as friends. I don't even want a boyfriend right now, anyway."

"Face it," Lexie said. "You're too much woman for him, Jess. I've always thought that, but I didn't say so. He and Danielle are perfect for each other. I mean, they're both straight arrows, and neither one of them wants to rush a relationship."

"They are perfect," Jessica agreed. "This is a relief. I've been nervous about Luke. When you learn someone doesn't have the same feelings for you anymore, it can hurt."

"I know," I said, my voice and shoulders dropping.

"Okay, Jeffrey's another story," Lexie interjected. "You've

got him right where you want him, begging for you to take him back. So what're you gonna do, Miss Matchmaker?"

I shrugged. "I don't know."

"My advice?" Lexie offered. "Take him back. You've had your fun and strung him along, but don't play him for too long or you run the risk of losing him for good."

"Take him back?" I stammered. I wanted to, but I was afraid.

"Yes," Lexie stressed. "Anna, Jeffrey never stopped liking you. He's just hard-core about this wrestling stuff. You can deal with that. You could have a guy who's got much bigger faults than that, trust me."

I wondered if she was referring to her dad, who I knew wasn't a good man. "What's your situation with Peter, then?" I pushed. Two could play her game, plus I was stalling because I wasn't sure I was ready to talk to Jeffrey.

"Peter's a pain, but he's careful with my heart," Lexie said. "He's going to be my husband someday. I've got it all planned out."

Jessica and I glanced at each other with wide eyes. "Does he know that?" I asked.

"I've got him on a need-to-know basis, and he doesn't need to know that detail just yet. You, on the other hand, need to talk to Jeffrey now," Lexie stressed again, bringing our conversation back to me. How did she do that?

"She's right," Jessica agreed. "Go find him."

"I don't know," I said, stalling. "I'm not sure this is the best time. Look what happened the last time I tried talking to him after he lost."

"Go!" they ordered.

"Okay," I said, throwing my hands in the air. I pushed back in my chair, but that was as far as I made it because Danielle came walking up to our table—and Mr. Terupt was with her.

Danielle

I bumped into Mr. Terupt on my way back from the bathroom.

"Danielle," he said. "I was just coming to say goodbye to all of you. Where is everyone?"

"I think Lexie and Jessica are sitting at one of the tables near the concessions area. Anna was still in the gym last I saw her."

"Let's go see," he said.

We walked down the hallway, and when we turned the corner I spotted all three of the girls sitting together. "Look who I found," I said, sidling up to their table.

"Hi," they sang in chorus.

"Actually, I'm here to say goodbye," Mr. Terupt replied. "I need to get going, but I'll see you in school. Now that wrestling is finished, we need to get serious about our haircuts."

We smiled.

"Did you see Jeffrey or Peter?" Anna asked. "Are they really upset?"

"I saw Jeffrey," Mr. Terupt said. "Yes, he's upset, but he's okay. Peter still won't come near me," he added, his voice dropping.

"That's it," Lexie snapped. "I'm gonna kick his butt way worse than it got kicked today."

"That's sweet of you, Lexie, but I'm afraid that won't help," Mr. Terupt said. "No butt kicking is going to heal Peter's heart. That needs time and it has to happen on its own."

"It better happen soon, then!" Lexie spat. "I'm running out of patience."

"I hope so," Mr. Terupt said. "Bye, girls."

"Bye," we responded.

We watched him walk out of the school and then Lexie said, "I still might kick Peter's butt."

"Not today," Jessica replied. "My mom just texted; she's waiting for us out front."

Anna and I gave them hugs and headed to get our coats from the bleachers because our ride would be here next—except we ran into Luke as he was coming out of the gym.

"I'll get yours," Anna said, slipping past him and disappearing inside, leaving the two of us standing there.

"Are you leaving?" I asked.

"Yes, my mom is on her way." He was staring at the floor and scuffing his foot back and forth. Why wouldn't he look at me?

"I've gotta go," I blurted, hurrying into the gym. Suddenly, I felt hot and dizzy. I needed space so I could breathe again. What had Anna said to him? And had she also talked to Jessica?

Jeffrey

"Jeffrey, can you take your brother to get something small from the concessions now? I'm not sure he can wait any longer. He's been asking all day," Mom said.

"Sure," I agreed. "C'mon, Ash."

I took my little brother's hand and led the way. I continued watching the wrestling as we walked, so I didn't see who was coming toward us—but Asher did.

"Anna," he squealed. He slipped his hand free from mine and ran to her, wrapping his arms around her in a double-leg attack.

"Hi, Asher," she said, bending over and hugging him back.

When they let go of their hug Asher took Anna's hand and pulled her closer to me. He reached out and took my hand next. Then he mushed my hand and Anna's hand together, patting them for good measure. I looked at Anna, my heart racing. A storm of relief and happiness and hope and so much more surged through my body when she gave my hand a squeeze. Her fingers slid in between mine and interlocked. Asher smiled at us like he'd just won the State Championship.

Part of me felt like there was still a lot I needed to say to her—which there was—but another part felt like everything had just been said. The best move wasn't any takedown or reversal that day, it was Asher putting us back together— the way we belonged.

Danielle

I held it together on the car ride home and I made it through dinner, but as soon as we had the table cleared and the dishes done, I marched Anna straight to my bedroom.

"Did you say something to Luke?" I asked before exploding.

"Maybe. Why?"

"Anna, now is not the time to play cat and mouse. I can't take it. Did you say something to him or not?"

"He likes you," she replied.

"What do you mean he likes me?"

"I mean he likes-you, likes-you, Danielle."

"Are you sure?"

"Yes, I'm sure!" she exclaimed.

I opened my mouth, but nothing came out. I'd never had

anyone like-me, like-me before. I felt tingly with excitement, and it wasn't my sugars. Anna grasped my hands and a huge smile spread across my face. We broke into a spontaneous dance, which ended in one of our classic giggle fits.

After our teenage-girl moment, Anna filled me in on all the details of her talk with Luke—and with Jessica. And then she told me what had happened with Jeffrey, which was one of the sweetest stories I'd ever heard. We were giggling again when there was a knock on my door and Grandma entered. She wiggled her bottom in between Anna and me and plopped down on my bed.

"So tell me, have you girls got this boy stuff straightened out yet?" she asked.

How did she know?

"You didn't think you could get that by me, did you?" she snickered. "Luke didn't keep coming over here for the cows, Danielle. I hope you didn't think that. The boy's serious about his schoolwork, I know, but most of his observations were about you."

Anna snorted. True to form, Grandma hadn't missed one beat.

"Now listen," she instructed. "Adolescent boys can be the dumbest creatures on God's green earth. Isn't that right, Anna?"

Anna nodded, but I could see her wondering how Grandma knew about Jeffrey.

"But they can be surprisingly sweet and sensitive at times too," Grandma continued. "What's important here is that you girls continue to look out for one another. And if you need any guidance, you can try praying—and this is no knock against our Lord—but you're better off talking to a woman about this stuff, so I'm always here if you need me."

Grandma patted our knees and then got up and made her way to my door.

"Thank you, Grandma," I said.

She glanced back and gave us a wink before leaving. Then Anna and I looked at each other and said the same thing at the same time: "Lexie."

When Grandma said that part about "you're better off talking to a woman about this stuff," Lexie came to mind immediately. That was definitely something she'd say. Lexie was always there to help us—with dresses, Polar Plunges, boys, anything and everything—but she was the one who needed us now. It was our turn to be there for her. The head-shaving event was next and that was Lexie's main concern. Why?

"Do you think her GeneLink results really arrived?" Anna asked.

"That's exactly what I was wondering," I said. "I don't know. It's possible."

We had asked her and she'd said no, but now we were starting to have our doubts. Lexie was an experienced liar, and she wouldn't be lying to hurt us, but because she had the results and . . . It was almost too scary to imagine.

Anna and I hadn't teamed up on God in a while, but we kneeled by my bed and hit Him with one of our tag-team prayers. There was a lot going on down here that we needed Him paying attention to.

"Dear God it's me, Danielle."

"And me," Anna said. "The first people we want to pray for are the babies on board, the one in Mrs. Terupt's belly and the one in Mom's—my future brother or sister. Please keep an eye on them."

"So far so good, so keep up the strong work," I added.

Anna giggled. I continued.

"Next, we'd like to pray for Peter. He is having a very hard time with Mr. Terupt moving. Maybe you can send him a sign or something that will help heal his heart like Mr. Terupt mentioned.

"And last, but definitely not least, we pray for Lexie. Please forgive us if we've been bad friends. We forgot about her GeneLink test and now we're worried she might have her results. We pray that you can guide her and help her with those decisions.

"God, we understand you might not be able to answer all of our prayers, but we have faith in you. And just so you know, Anna and I plan to do whatever we can to make the head-shaving event a smash hit—for Lexie's mother and all people affected by breast cancer out there. And for Lexie. You're more than welcome to help us with that too. Amen."

"Amen," Anna repeated.

Peter

Instead of going to the library during advising, I decided to pay Principal Lee another visit. I didn't want to be around T, but that didn't mean I couldn't still help the gang.

"Mr. Jacobs, to what do I owe today's surprise visit?" Mr. Lee said when I walked into his office.

I took a seat in the chair opposite his desk, the same one I always sat in, just not as much this year. "Hey, Mr. Lee. Let me get right to the point. We—me and the gang—are starting work on our next project. We want to hold a head-shaving event to raise money for breast cancer."

He leaned forward. "Did you have a date in mind?"

Not the question I was expecting. "Umm . . . no."

"Okay, let's have a look and see if we can find one, then." He pulled up the master calendar on his laptop. I watched his eyes as he scanned the screen. "Here," he said, stabbing his finger at the computer. "Friday, April tenth, right before vacation. There's nothing else on the calendar, and there probably won't be much happening in your classrooms. We'll invite the whole school and have it in the gym. You can tell your friends."

"Wow. Thanks, Mr. Lee. But I actually came to ask you something else."

He eyed me suspiciously. "Okay. What?"

"Will you agree to participate?"

"You mean shave my head?" he roared.

"Yeah," I said, nodding enthusiastically. "You were cool with doing the Polar Plunger, so why not this? If we raise enough dough, will you do it?"

"Tell me, Mr. Jacobs: What has prompted the sudden projects? First the Polar Plunger, as you call it, and now this."

"That's just how things are with Mr. Terupt. Now you know why we fought so hard to save him. He's the bes—" I stopped short, having just realized what I was saying. "*Was* the best," I mumbled.

"Yes, it's too bad he'll be leaving after this year. I can see you're still struggling with that."

I shrugged. "Whatever," I grumbled.

Mr. Lee stared at me—and kept staring. I shifted in my chair.

"Have you and the gang thought of doing anything special for him before he goes?"

"That's what these projects are supposed to be," I explained. "This is our makeshift bucket list with him. It was Luke's idea. He's all about projects."

"Bucket list?" Mr. Lee repeated. "Does that mean I should expect more events? What's next?"

I shrugged. "I don't know."

"Well, you can tell your gang and Mr. Terupt that I've agreed to participate in this one. If you can raise the dough, then I'll shave my head in front of a packed gymnasium."

"Really?"

"Yes. You might say Mr. Terupt has inspired me, but the truth is, so has your gang, Mr. Jacobs. You kids are great with him, but you can be great without him too."

"Thanks, Mr. Lee," I said, jumping to my feet. "I'll let them know."

"Mr. Jacobs, one more thing before you go."

I stopped.

"Did you watch the movie?"

"*Hoosiers?* Yeah, it was a cool flick—even for a basketball story. Did you know it's considered one of the best sports movies of all time?"

"I did, but that's not why I gave it to you."

"Why did you give it to me?" I asked.

"Do you remember Everett, the young man who had the alcoholic father?"

"Yeah, why?"

"Did you see how their relationship changed over the course of the movie, and how it was love and understanding that helped both of them in the end?"

I nodded.

"Regret is hard to live with, Mr. Jacobs. And if you watch this beloved teacher of yours leave when you're still feeling angry with him, I'm afraid you'll regret it. I don't want to see you make that mistake."

I turned and left. I didn't know what to say, and I couldn't talk with the sudden knot in my throat choking me. I got out of there.

LUKE

**IF it is discovered that your romantic feelings
are mutual,
THEN flirting is the next phase.**

With a successful Polar Plunge under our belts and wrestling now officially over for the season, we came to advising with one objective: it was time to get serious about Lexie's head-shaving event. We hadn't done anything to prepare for it yet. None of the details or logistics were ironed out, so there was tons to do, and we got started immediately.

Anna and Jeffrey sat at a computer and got cracking on the rough outline for a flier, while Danielle pulled out the construction paper and pencils and markers and began making posters. And before I knew it Lexie and Jessica had teamed up with Mr. Terupt and were investigating how to make this a fundraising event for the Breast Cancer Research Foundation. I had thought I would do that, but this was Lexie's thing, so I didn't object.

"Luke, we've got this, so why don't you go see if Danielle needs some help?" Lexie suggested.

I froze. Jessica was busy looking at something on the computer with Mr. Terupt and didn't even flinch. I didn't know whether she hadn't heard Lexie or didn't care. I glanced at Anna and she nodded excitedly, like Lexie's suggestion was a good one, so maybe she had talked to Jessica. When I turned back to Lexie she got up and pushed me toward Danielle. "Go," she whispered. "It's okay."

Gulp. This was so much easier when we didn't know we liked each other. I took a deep breath and walked over and sat next to Danielle at Mr. Terupt's worktable. She peeked up at me and smiled. I smiled back. She already had a good start on a head-shaving sketch.

"You're so good at drawing," I said.

"Thanks," she whispered.

I felt like I could sit and watch her hands for the rest of advising. I was under the spell of some invisible force, and it had me wanting to slide closer to her. But there was a stronger invisible force holding me back—the chicken one.

"Can you help me make a list of all the things we're going to need for this event while you keep working, or will that distract you?" I asked.

"No, I can do both," she said.

I opened my notebook and then I reached into the bin for something to write with. Danielle had reached for a marker at the same instant. Our hands touched. We let them linger there, our fingers tangling together.

"Chairs or stools," Danielle said.

My face scrunched.

"For your list," she explained.

"Oh," I said. Slowly, I pulled my hand away. I wrote down *chairs or stools* on my list. Together, we thought to add clippers, razors, scissors, brooms, aprons, and extension cords. We didn't have everything listed, but we had a good start when Peter suddenly burst into the classroom.

"I have great news," he announced.

Everyone stopped and looked, surprised to see him.

"I just met with Principal Lee. He put our head-shaving event on the school calendar for Friday, April tenth, right before we go on vacation. He reserved the gym for us because he wants to make this an all-school event."

"Peter, that's terrific!" Jessica exclaimed.

"Yeah, and that's not even the best part," Peter said. "Mr. Lee has agreed to shave his head in front of the whole school if we raise enough cash."

"No way!" I yelled, jumping to my feet, unable to contain my excitement. This was huge. It was just the thing we needed to put us over the edge.

"Way," Peter promised.

"This is going to be epic!" I said.

The gang laughed and we got back to work, completely energized by Peter's news. It was time to get serious, but when I sat down I saw something that made my insides do loop-de-loops. A tiny heart had been added at the bottom of my list.

Alexia

Like, you can't say Teach didn't try, because he did. After Peter burst into advising with his big announcement, and after Luke got done going all cheerleader on us, Teach tried.

"Great work, Peter," he said.

But Peter didn't say anything. Didn't even acknowledge Teach.

That was the last straw. Teach had said kicking Peter's butt wouldn't do any good, that Peter's heart had to heal on its own, but I knew a thing or two about Peter's heart. So I grabbed him by the elbow and pulled him into the hall. I knew there were eyes on us, but no one said a word.

"What's up?" Peter said, acting like he didn't already know.

I took his hands in mine. "Thank you for getting Principal Lee involved and for helping to make my event special."

He smiled. "Don't act surprised. You know I'd do any-thing for you."

"Good, because there is something else that I need you to do."

"What?"

"Stop being angry at Teach. You need to forgive him. He's trying to hide it, but like, you've got him hurting bad. Not to mention the gang is all wrong without you."

"*He's* hurting?" Peter scoffed. "You want me to feel bad *for him*? It's his fault!"

"Peter—"

"No," he snapped, cutting me off. "I wish you hadn't asked me to do the one thing I can't. I'm sorry."

He dropped my hands and left me standing there. I stared at his back as he walked down the hall and disap-peared around the corner.

If Teach was able to forgive Peter for throwing that snowball, why couldn't Peter forgive him for moving away? Peter's heart wasn't that cold. It was that broken.

Jessica

I told . . .
Lexie's mother
at the restaurant where she waitressed
when I made the trip with my father
one afternoon.

Dad and I
sat in a booth
and Lexie's mother
took our orders.

"It's very nice to meet you, Mr. Writeman," she said.
The pleasure is mine, Dad replied.
"You have a remarkable daughter here."
Thank you, Dad said. *I know.*

But Lexie's mother
didn't know
about her own remarkable daughter,
so I had to tell her.
I'd debated
doing it
long enough.

Sometimes being a friend
requires doing something
for that friend
that she can't do
for herself.

I left Dad sitting in the booth
and went and found Miss Johnson,
and I told her
about GeneLink
and the results
Lexie still hadn't opened.
She needed to know.
Lexie needed her to know.

After the truth
had spilled from inside me,
Miss Johnson's hand flew to her mouth,
trapping the gasp from escaping
and making too much noise.

Shock,
pain,
and sorrow
mixed together on her face.

Then rapid-fire questions:
"How did she get that kit?
When did she do it?
How long has she had the results?"

"Miss Johnson, please don't ask me questions
that I can't answer."

"What should I do?"
was a question
I could answer.
"Be there for our head-shaving event," I said.

She nodded.
And then she told me something
that I needed to hear.

"Jessica, it's okay to forgive your father,
even if your mother can't."

april

Alexia

Peter still wasn't cool with Teach, but he did start coming to advising. I was hoping for more, but this was a start, so I didn't push it. Advising wasn't exactly a time to chill anyways, though it did seem to be a time for Luke and Danielle to flirt, which was super cute, by the way. But seriously, we were, like, totes busy trying to get everything ready for our head-shaving event. The gang was determined to make this another huge success, just like our Polar Plunge had been.

To raise money, we had a table set up before school and during lunch where students and teachers could donate to our cause. We were going to take turns woman-ing the station, but no one wanted to miss out, so like, we were all there every day. The problem was we weren't getting much action. Things were slow and I was getting depressed, but then Luke came up with this super smart way to get everyone excited to donate, and all of a sudden we were swamped.

Luke asked Danielle to whip up a large poster with all of our faces on it—the gang's and Teach's and Principal Lee's. Then he drew a tall bar on it, like one of those you see on graphs, under each face. At the bottom of each bar he wrote $XXX. After that, when students or teachers donated, we asked them whose head they wanted the money to go to. We gradually colored in the bars as the cash came in. When the goal amount was reached, the bar would be filled in, which meant that person could say goodbye to their hair. The reason Luke put $XXX instead of an actual number was because he didn't know how much we could actually raise, and he didn't want to aim too low or too high. It turned out having the amount stay a mystery encouraged more donations, because as long as the bar was progressing, kids kept donating.

So like, things were going really well and I was totes excited—until the big day drew closer and I saw what was happening. I know we all said back in the beginning we'd do it, but like, talk was cheap. Back then there was no face attached to the donations, so it didn't feel real. But it was real now. Everybody wanted to see Principal Lee bald, so they were dumping money to his name left and right. Luke wouldn't shut up about how it was going to be epic. Unfortunately, there was also a contingent of students who thought seeing girls bald—especially me!—would be epic too.

LUKE

IF you make an event epic,
THEN people will remember it, talk about it,
and want to do it again.

I wondered if Lexie had stopped to consider the conse-
quences, but I didn't want to talk her out of it. Her being
bald was one of the keys to making the event epic. But when
the reality of saying goodbye to her precious hair started to
sink in, she began to crack. The girls tried consoling her,
but believe it or not, it really was Peter who helped the most
this time.

"Don't worry, Lex. Lukester made the amount of dough
for your head a mystery, so we can just say your goal was
never reached. You don't need to shave your head." He
scoffed, trying to make Lexie feel better.

Technically, Peter was right. Lying would've been easy in this case. But surprisingly, Lexie didn't want to cheat.

"I have to do it," she said. "This event is for my mom and all of the women and families who've been affected by breast cancer—and for me."

She made it sound like it was definitely happening. "If you *and* Principal Lee do this, it really will be epic!" I exclaimed, getting excited. "And then people will want to do it again. This doesn't have to be a one-timer, Lexie. You can make this something special. You can make a difference."

"Thanks," she mumbled.

"And you *have* raised the most money," I pointed out.

"That's it. I don't care how much money I raise. If she's doing it then so am I," Peter declared. He wasn't done trying to make Lexie feel better.

Lexie gave a weak smile. "For such a dummy, you can be really sweet sometimes," she said.

"You can count on me too," Jeffrey said. "I've got your back. I told you I'd do it, and I will. This poster didn't change that."

"Me too," Jessica echoed.

"And us," Danielle and Anna followed.

"How 'bout it, Lukester?" Peter asked, putting me on the spot. "You in? It's going to be *epic*."

I'd been excited when it was just Lexie and Principal Lee, but excited was the last thing I was feeling now. I glanced at Danielle. She was waiting for my response.

> **IF you have feelings for a girl,**
> **THEN you will do anything for her.**

"I'm in," I croaked.

Danielle smiled.

"Atta boy, Lukester!" Peter crowed. "A bald brainiac."

I reached up and ran my fingers through my hair.

> **IF you want to know if someone truly likes you,**
> **THEN shave your head and wait to see**
> **if they run away or stick around.**

"You can count on me too," a surprise voice said behind us.

We spun around to find Mr. Terupt standing there. "Can't be a bucket-list event if I'm not involved."

I did a fist pump. Epic, I thought.

Peter

I helped with the fundraising table and spreading the word for the event. I even volunteered to shave my head. I did everything I could for Lexie's event—everything except the one thing she had asked for. I couldn't. It was going to be way easier to see T go if I was mad at him—plain and simple. If he was still the guy I loved, then saying goodbye was going to rip my heart out.

But if what Principal Lee had said was true, regret was bound to gnaw at my heart for the rest of my days. Still, I couldn't help the way I felt. Having T move was no different than having him dead. I could believe that junk about regret, but I wasn't kidding myself by believing we'd ever see the guy again. I wasn't falling for that—not for one second. The truth was, we weren't ever going to see him again, because that's how the real world works—and that was on him. Moving away and forgetting about us was his choice— and being pissed about it was mine.

But here was the catch: I couldn't convince myself that the guy didn't care about us—no matter how hard I tried. He was there for Jeffrey and me at our tournaments, even though I refused to talk to him, and he did the Polar Plunger and even agreed to shave his head. It was that last move that proved to be my breaking point.

Danielle

Shaving my head wasn't going to be easy, but it also wasn't going to be permanent—not like how my pancreas quitting on me was. Hair grows back. At least, that was what I kept reminding myself. I'd thought I was prepared, but Grandma knew better.

It was at Sunday dinner when Anna and I first informed the family of our plans at Lexie's event, and once Grandma heard, she insisted on attending—for support. She left it at that until she had us alone, helping her with the dishes, and then she told us how it was going to be.

"Are the two of you blinded by love already, or is it your faith?" Grandma asked. She didn't wait for our responses, and that was okay because we didn't know how to answer.

"It's good you've got the Lord behind you, make no mistake about that," she continued, "but you'll need more than Him when they come at you with those clippers. I'll be there. Don't you worry."

Her stern look was all the proof we needed to know she wasn't fooling. Grandma hung her dishrag on the oven and left Anna and me standing in the kitchen.

"Don't worry?" I whispered. "I'm more worried about her being there than not being there. What does she think she's going to do?"

Anna shrugged. "Guess we'll have to wait and see."

That wasn't very comforting, either, but Anna and I soon discovered having Grandma in the gym on the day of the head-shaving event was. When those first clippers started buzzing I was shaking worse than if I had a low blood sugar. The crowd watching might've been hooting and cheering and laughing, but none of us sitting on the stage were. I did a quick scan of the bleachers and spotted Grandma. As promised, she was there. Her mere presence gave me the courage and strength I needed. I steeled myself.

Poor Lexie, on the other hand, was a different story. Not even Grandma being there could help her. We'd tried telling her she didn't need to do it. I was certain if we'd said her name hadn't raised enough money God would've let that lie slide, but Lexie refused. Her stubbornness could've rivaled even Grandma's, but stubbornness wasn't enough to get her through.

I'd never experienced nor witnessed a panic attack before, but I was almost certain Lexie started having one. She didn't look good. She turned white as milk and began struggling to breathe, fighting to catch her breath. Someone had to do something. She was in trouble.

anna

Lexie wasn't pulling out, but she also wasn't breathing very well. Something needed to be done before she passed out—or worse. Danielle bowed her head and began praying, but that wasn't Peter's style. He stood in front of the crowd and made a bold announcement. "It's time to get this party started! I'm going first!"

If Lexie could've talked maybe she would've objected. But before that happened Jeffrey stepped next to Peter and yelled, "Me too!" And you might not believe this, but Luke was not to be outdone. He walked over and joined his buddies and the three of them raised their fists in the air. It reminded me of how everyone came together at the sit-in last year.

"They volunteer as tribute!" some kid in the bleachers squawked.

319

That was all it took for everyone in the gym to go bon-
kers. People were screaming and cheering. Me? I had to wipe
my eyes. Not because I was scared. But because I knew exactly what Lexie would say. For being such dummies, they
could be the sweetest guys in the whole world.

It didn't take long for Peter to remind us he was a
dummy, though.

Peter

After Jeffrey and Lukester joined me and volunteered their heads with mine, the gym broke into pandemonium. I'm not kidding. It was like a rock concert. I jogged to the center stool and sat down.

"Hurry up before I change my mind," I urged Barber Joe.

I'd done crazy before, but this took the cake. Barber Joe cranked that electric razor up to full blast. I was pissing my pants, but I didn't move a muscle. If wrestling had taught me anything, it was how to be mentally tough. If T had taught me anything, it was how to have my friends' backs—and I had Lexie's. I gritted my teeth and Barber Joe took that thing and ran it right down the middle of my head, giving me a big stripe. The crowd erupted into wild cheering. There was no backing out now.

It didn't take Barber Joe long to finish the job. When he was done I reached up and felt my buzzed scalp.

"Hey, Cue Ball!" some punk hollered, which prompted a slew of shouts and cheers and more catcalls.

My legs felt dead but I managed to stand, and then Jeffrey plopped down right behind me. He knew about having backs too—and right now he had mine. Barber Joe's razor fired up again but I didn't stick around to watch. Suffering from shock, I stumbled like a mummy to the side and found my backpack. I reached inside and pulled out the bottle of aftershave I'd taken from Dad's bathroom cabinet that morning. I dumped a good splash onto my hand and began rubbing it around—spell broken!

That crap burned so bad it felt like my head was on fire. It was even worse than the chemical burns I got from the beard dye back in seventh grade. I would like to know who came up with the brilliant idea of calling it *aftershave*, because no person in their right mind would put that stuff on after shaving. It was torture!

I bounded into the bleachers and grabbed the first water bottle I spotted and poured it over my head. Relief. I sighed. I was soaked, but I felt better. Only then did I realize the gym was staring and laughing at me, but I didn't care. When I glanced back at the gang, I saw Lexie with teary eyes—and she was smiling. That was all that mattered. It was worth it.

I climbed down the bleachers and joined the others.

"Peter, we're only just getting started and you've already made this epic," Lukester said.

"Not until you shave your head," I reminded him. "You're next."

Luke's body stiffened. With all the excitement, he'd forgotten he was also participating. Jeffrey and I sat our project leader on the stool and stayed by his side for moral support. When Barber Joe finished and clicked off the razor, Lukester got up from the stool and the gym erupted into cheers again. Slowly, he turned to Jeffrey and me and his face broke into a huge smile. He'd just gotten a taste of what it felt like to score a winning takedown late in the match and have the crowd going wild for you.

I slapped some of Dad's aftershave on his head. I didn't want him to feel left out. And then Lukester danced like a chicken.

"Congratulations, Lukester. You just made this epic," I said, and laughed.

But we weren't done yet. There was more to come.

Jeffrey

My new haircut was a good look for wrestling, so getting it done wasn't that hard for me, but I understood it wasn't the same for everyone else. It was funny when Peter went. And funnier still when he put that aftershave on his head and then on Luke's. There was whistling and shouting and friendly banter—but there was none of that with the girls. When it was their turn, it wasn't funny. It was serious. But that was good, because cancer isn't a joke. I knew that and Lexie knew that—all too well. And thanks to our head-shaving event, I think everyone in the gym got a tiny glimpse of that before we were done.

Danielle

When it was our turn, we didn't go one at a time like the boys had. We had exactly four stools and four stylists from Lexie's hair salon. The girls and I sat close enough that we could hold hands, and then we stared straight ahead.

First, the stylists braided our hair, and then with one quick snip, it was gone. That was the portion of our hair we got to donate, which was something we could be proud of, just not right then. I was much too scared to feel proud. They turned the electric razors on and the girls and I squeezed hands. I don't think there was a breath taken anywhere in the gym for the duration of the buzzing.

When the last of the clippers fell silent and our last hair had fallen, the four of us stood on trembling legs and took a bow. Only then did the gym come to life again.

"Freak Show presents: the Four Baldies!" some jerk cat-called and whistled, thinking he was funny. He got more than he bargained for.

Grandma turned on him faster than a rattlesnake. She climbed the bleachers and grabbed that boy by his shirt collar. Rumor has it she threatened to drag him to the floor and shave his head and eyebrows herself, but I've never actually asked her what she said and she's never told. Whatever it was, it worked, because that boy wasn't laughing or poking fun after that. And something just as unexpected happened next.

There was a slow rise in murmurs all around Grandma, spreading throughout the bleachers. That was followed by clapping, soft at first, but quickly growing into raucous applause, ending in a standing ovation—for Grandma and the Four Baldies. We didn't need to worry about being harassed after that. I felt Anna squeeze my hand.

Thanks be to God—but more to Grandma.

Alexia

After Danielle's grandma kicked some major butt we got a standing O. And then we walked to the side of our staging area and Mom was there waiting for me. She wrapped me in a seriously tight hug.

"I'm so proud of you, honey," she whispered, squeezing me hard. She held me close for a few seconds before easing up. "Remember how you helped me stay stylish when it was me? Well, now it's your turn." She pulled a scarf from her purse and covered my head. She knotted it in the back and then spun me around to look at me again. She leaned in and kissed my forehead. "So proud," she whispered.

"Mom, I've got to tell you something," I said. Shaving my head had left me exposed. It was time to open up.

"What is it?" she asked, nervousness in her voice.

"I used this home DNA test kit called GeneLink, to see if I have the cancer gene."

"I know," Mom said, her voice cracking.

Jessica, I thought. But instead of getting mad, I felt relief. "My results are at home, but I haven't opened them. I don't think I'm ready yet. I'm scared."

"We can wait as long as you want. Cancer is scary. It's also not something you fight on your own, Alexia. You find strength in the people around you, the ones who love you."

"I didn't want you to worry."

"That's my job. We're in this together," Mom said. "Always. No matter what."

"And I'm with both of you," Vincent said, pulling us close. He must've arrived during all the excitement—after swinging by the barber shop.

He was bald and Mom was crying. What a sight we must've been.

Jessica

I see . . .
Lexie
hugging her mom
and Vincent.
Her gaze falls on me
and she mouths the words,
thank you.

I see
my mom
and dad
looking at me,
with admiration.
They're proud

of their bald daughter.
The one they each had a part
in making (gross!),
and in raising.

I see
my mom
and dad
join hands,
and my heart flies
almost out of my chest.

I see
that what I hope for
might be possible
again
in the future.

I see
that it's time
for our head-shaving
grand finale
after I hear
Mr. Lee's pronouncement,
the part you've all been waiting for.

Peter

After everyone in the place had their moment to be all sentimental and emotional over the girls, Principal Lee took the microphone and shook things up again.

"And now," he bellowed, "the part you've all been waiting for!"

He did a badass mic drop and then he and T made a show and strutted like two gangsters over to Barber Joe's stool. Next to Lexie, Lee had raised the most money, so we saved his head for the grand finale. And since T was the only other adult getting shaved, he joined Mr. Lee and went first.

Let me just say, those two had the crowd in a wild frenzy. After all, it's not every day that you get to watch your principal and teacher get their heads shaved. Still, I didn't care.

I was done with T—but then something happened that cracked my shield and split me wide open.

Barber Joe's razor fired up for one last round. Hair started falling and hoots and howls bounced off the walls. Barber Joe circled to his left, working his way around T's head, and that was when I saw it—the scar. A scar that brought me all the way back to fifth grade.

Jeffrey

When Terupt was done and stood and faced us, that was it. There was no hesitation. Peter ran across the floor and hugged him. Finally, we had the gang back the way it was supposed to be. The way it would always be.

I glanced at my friends, who all wore the same happy and relieved expressions. Together, we walked over and joined Peter and Terupt. The hoots and hollers and cheering quieted. The crowd must've been completely confused by what they were witnessing—all except for one group of students who definitely got it.

Principal Lee had made this an all-school event, which meant our class of students with special needs was also there. Back at Snow Hill School it was the Collaborative Classroom. I didn't know what it was called at the junior high. I rarely saw these kids. But they were here now. And they were still clapping and cheering. And then one of the boys came and hugged us. No one had a bigger heart than my brother Michael, and this boy reminded me of him.

"You came around just in time," I told Peter. "I know what we're going to do for our bucket-list event." The idea had come to me all at once—and it was perfect.

"What is it?" Luke asked, already eager for his next project.

"Yeah, what is it?" Peter echoed.

I was about to fill them in when the gym exploded with a final round of screams and shouts. I swear, I thought the roof was going to come off the place. We turned and looked. Principal Lee was now Principal Clean.

LUKE

IF you're patient and keep thinking,
THEN eventually you will figure it out.

When all was said and done, and the gym had emptied and it was just Mr. Terupt and us, we took a minute to laugh with each other about our new looks, but only for a minute, because Jeffrey was excited to tell us his idea.

"We're going to put together a wrestling event for kids with special needs. Peter and I will get our team involved so that we can hold a couple of practices to teach the kids the rules and a few basic moves. And then we'll have a night when we host a special match, when each wrestler from our team will go against one of our special needs athletes, giving them a chance to show what they've learned and be the star."

There was still a lot left to figure out, but we had the general idea—and we loved it! Jeffrey's heart was on full display with this one.

On our way out of the gym, Peter summed it up perfectly.

"Well, Lukester, you can chalk today up as epic. Pretty sure this was a date that will be remembered forever."

A date that will be remembered forever, I thought. That was it. Jeffrey wasn't the only one to have his bucket-list idea take him by surprise. I thought of mine now too. Jeffrey and Peter's wrestling event needed to happen first, but I knew what I was doing. And it was going to be exactly what we needed.

may

ANNA

The bucket-list events had been everything we'd hoped for so far—important, memorable, and bigger than us— and I knew Jeffrey's idea would be no different. But before we could tackle that project, there was something else we needed to do. And that something else was one of my favorite jobs.

One afternoon in early May, Mr. Terupt needed help from the Babysitters Gang. He was taking Mrs. Terupt to her routine checkup on Baby Terupt Number Two. I was excited to watch Hope again, but between Mrs. Terupt's growing belly and all the moving boxes that seemed to have suddenly appeared throughout their house, the end was clearly in sight, and that had me feeling anything but excited— and, as I soon found out, I wasn't the only one feeling that way. One look at our bald heads and Hope started crying.

"Holy smokes, we're so ugly we scared her," Peter quipped.

"Don't take it personally," Mr. Terupt said. "She did that when I first came home too."

"It's okay, Hope. It's just us. *Polar Bear, Polar Bear*," Jessica sang. "Remember?"

That did the trick. Hope stopped crying and smiled at Jessica with big eyes. Jessica took her from Mrs. Terupt and we followed them upstairs to our usual spot. Mr. and Mrs. Terupt used that chance to quietly slip away.

I helped Jessica get Hope settled on her play mat and then we sat beside her with a stack of books. It didn't take long before Lexie broke the ice and I discovered Hope and I weren't the only ones dealing with uneasy feelings.

"Do you guys think we'll keep getting together like this after Teach is gone?" she asked.

"Don't say gone," Jessica objected. "Say moved away. Gone sounds too permanent."

"Fine. Whatever," Lexie huffed. "Do you think we'll keep getting together like this after he's moved away?"

"Oh, no," Peter balked. "No you don't. That's exactly what I was saying all along and you guys were giving me grief. And now that I've come to terms with it, you're trying to drag me back there. No way."

"But will we?" Lexie persisted, voicing all of our fears. "And like, how do we know?"

"We don't," Jeffrey answered. "There are no guarantees in life. We've all seen that. Diabetes. Cancer. You just never know. But if sticking together is truly important to us, then we'll make it happen."

"We're going to make it happen," Luke said. "Don't worry." He sounded so confident, but offered no explanation on how we were going to do it.

"This is when faith and prayer become important," Danielle reasoned.

"Yeah, you say that, but like, how in the world am I supposed to know if God is listening or tuning me out?" Lexie asked.

"That's the faith part," Danielle replied. "God answers in mysterious ways. You have to believe in that, but you can't spend all of your time worrying about it. We need to live in the present and enjoy it while we've got it. At least, that's what Grandma says."

"Your grandma's awesome!" Peter exclaimed. "She had that loudmouth seventh-grader crapping his pants. That was so funny."

"Grandma Roberts is the best," I agreed.

"Yeah," Peter continued. "So, like she says, we need to enjoy today and have some fun instead of sitting around and holding a pout party."

"Okay, Mr. Let's Have a Good Time, what do you suggest?" Jeffrey challenged.

Peter took a second to glance around the room. "I've got it," he said, and grinned.

"Uh-oh," Luke replied.

"Uh-oh is right," Lexie agreed. "Whenever you have one

of your sudden brilliant ideas it's usually the opposite, totally dumb. Like when you thought peeing on my leg was going to be the answer."

"That wasn't dumb, that was romantic," Peter argued.

"Ohmigod," Lexie shrieked, throwing the couch pillow at him.

Peter ducked and Hope squealed.

"You two better stop. You're scaring Hope," Jeffrey said.

"She's not scared, she's entertained," Peter claimed.

"She's gonna be entertained when she watches me kick your butt," Lexie said.

"Will you let me share my idea, and then you can decide if it's dumb or not?" Peter asked.

"Yes, please tell us so we can move past this banter," Jessica pleaded.

Hope squealed again.

Peter smirked and then he filled us in. "I think we should hide seven different prizes in random moving boxes. One prize from each of us, and the prizes can be anything we want. When T and his darling bride are unpacking in their new home, they'll discover whatever we've left for them and smile—or yell," Peter added, and snickered.

We sat in silence because his idea wasn't dumb—at all. In fact, it was wonderful, but we were afraid to tell Peter that because then his head might not fit in the house anymore.

"Told you it was good," he bragged, strutting like a rooster after no one had objected.

"So what's your prize?" Jeffrey asked.

"Don't know yet," Peter admitted, "but I'll come up with something."

"Maybe we should leave artifacts?" Luke wondered.

"Artifacts? I like that," Jessica mused.

"Prizes or artifacts, whatever," Peter replied. "Just hide something."

"It doesn't need to be much," Jessica said. "A simple note or poem—"

"Or sketch," Danielle added.

"You guys can do that artifact stuff," Peter said. "I'm gonna try to come up with something else."

"Uh-oh," Luke replied.

"Uh-oh," Hope repeated, and we all laughed.

But uh-oh was right. Peter still had the potential to turn his wonderful idea into a disaster. Regardless, I was too excited about my artifact to worry about Peter.

I dug through my bag and found the spare thumb drive I was hoping for. Then I grabbed my computer, which I had with me because I hadn't been home since school let out, and then I sat down near Hope because we couldn't leave her all alone. I got busy sorting through all the photos I had saved on my computer, picking my best shots of the gang and Hope to copy to the thumb drive—my artifact. I folded a piece of paper into a makeshift envelope and stuck my artifact inside. On the outside, I wrote, *Pictures can be worth 1,000 words.* I taped the envelope closed and buried it inside one of the boxes.

I wasn't sure what anyone else decided to do, but this

might've been Peter's best idea ever. I didn't want Mr. Terupt to move, but I smiled thinking about him opening these moving boxes and discovering our random artifacts—assuming they were all something nice, like I had done.

Peter? He was the big unknown.

Danielle

Mrs. Writeman gave Anna and me a ride home after we babysat Hope. It wasn't dinnertime yet, but we found Mom and Grandma sitting at the table with Terri and Charlie when we walked into the house. They were waiting for us.

"What's wrong?" I asked, feeling their eyes on us the second we stepped through the door. "Where are Dad and Grandpa?"

"Everything's fine," Mom replied. "Your father and Grandpa—"

"Are doing chores," Grandma barked. "Charlie and Terri have something to tell us, but they wouldn't spill the beans until you two got home. 'Bout time. I was beginning to think I'd be in the ground before you decided to show up."

"Grandma, patience makes the world go round," I teased.

"And dead is permanent," she retorted, "so don't give me your hogwash. Now sit your rears in those chairs so we can finally hear what it is your brother and Terri have to say."

Grandma's sass had Anna and me giggling, but I did wonder what they could have to tell us that was so important. Everyone in the family already knew they were having a baby.

"Okay, what is it?" Grandma demanded once Anna and I sat down with them. She was long past having any patience.

"Charlie and I aren't having a baby," Terri said. "We're having three of them."

My eyes popped.

"Three!" Grandma hollered. "Holy cow!"

"Triplets?" Anna sputtered.

Terri and Charlie nodded.

"The Lord had better plan on keeping me around a while longer, 'cause you're gonna need lots of help with three," Grandma said.

Mom got up and hugged Terri and then Charlie.

"The Babysitters Gang lives on," Anna whispered.

I smiled. Exactly what I was thinking. The chances of having triplets had to be extremely rare, but the Lord works in mysterious ways.

LUKE

IF Mr. Terupt is involved,
THEN things don't slow down at the end of
the school year.

It never failed: when the end of the year drew closer, things got busier with Mr. Terupt. There was always important work to be done—and this year, like every year before it, felt like the most important yet.

If you've ever wondered what it means to go full circle, Jeffrey and Peter's wrestling idea was it. Our first interaction with students having special needs took place way back in the beginning, when Mr. Terupt had us visiting the Collaborative Classroom in fifth grade. And boy, did we learn a lot—about each other and ourselves. Now here we were as our time with Mr. Terupt continued winding down, finishing up with a project that highlighted students with special needs from the junior high school. That's going full circle. That was what made this another perfect bucket-list event. This endeavor showed just how much we'd grown and changed—because of Mr. Terupt.

By this stage in the game, we were a well-oiled machine when it came to organizing and running one of our bucket-list events. We were like a cell, each of us acting as an organelle, carrying out a vital function, but we also helped one another along the way.

Danielle was responsible for designing T-shirts. All the participants would get one, but we still didn't need that many, so we all pitched in a few dollars and placed the order. Anna was in charge of taking photographs at the event, but she also assisted Jessica and Lexie with the advertising and social media stuff. In addition, the girls needed to hand out medals to the participants after each of their matches. Again, we didn't need that many medals, so Mr. Terupt took care of ordering those. I was the emcee or play-by-play announcer. The guy with the microphone, in other words. Peter and Jeffrey and Mr. Terupt were the coaches. And Jeffrey and Peter were also participants.

To prepare for the event, the wrestling team held three practices after school. At those practices Jeffrey and Peter had each wrestler partner up with one special-needs athlete. Each athlete was taught a takedown, a turn from the top position, and an escape from the bottom. Jeffrey and Peter took time explaining and going over all the starting positions and rules. Everything was always reviewed at the next practice. I knew all this because I attended the practices to prepare for my role as emcee. I had a lot to learn as well if I expected to call a move by its correct name and understand the scoring.

By the time the big night rolled around, I knew it was going to be another event of epic proportions. And I was right. The stands were full with parents of special needs students along with members of the student body and school faculty and staff, all excited for the sixteen matches in our lineup. Wrestle'Lympics, as we decided to call it, was a night that gave you all the feels.

Peter

Obviously, it was different wrestling against Richie than it was against all of my other opponents. I was going to let him—even help him—execute the moves I'd shown him. Either I was a better coach than I realized or Richie knew something about having a game face, because he hit his double-leg harder than he ever had at practice. He buried his shoulder in my stomach and tackled me to the mat.

"There's a beautiful double-leg by Richie!" Luke yelled into his microphone.

The gym erupted with celebratory whistles and shouts. I was proud as heck and might've even smiled, but Richie had knocked the wind out of me—at both ends, if you know what I mean.

Richie heard it. And then he smelled it. And then he forgot all about having a game face and going for his moves.

He jumped off of me and started laughing and pointing. "Peter farted!" he yelled, plugging his nose. He turned and waved his hand back and forth behind his butt.

At this point everyone in the bleachers roared with laughter. My face burned with embarrassment.

"It appears Peter has farted," Luke, our brilliant play-by-play man, announced.

I glared and showed him my fist in warning. I wanted to run and hide, but there was no chance for that, because when I wasn't looking, Richie tackled me with another double. The place went bananas.

"There's another beautiful takedown for Richie!" Luke yelled.

The crowd cheered wildly and I smiled because they were done laughing at me and were rooting for Richie. And Richie didn't stop. He went right to work putting on the half-nelson I'd taught him and he pushed me over onto my back. I put on a show by bridging my shoulders off the mat, but Richie kept working, and eventually he got my back flat on the mat and the referee called the pin.

Richie sprang to his feet and raised his arms in victory. The boy had the biggest smile on his face I'd ever seen. Then he turned and gave me his hand and helped me up. He pulled me into a monster-sized hug. "I love you, Peter," he yelled into my ear.

I can't even begin to describe how special that made me feel. Even Jessica would struggle to find the right words for that.

"You're the best, Richie," I croaked.

Jeffrey

Wrestle'Lympics was an emotional night. We celebrated our special-needs athletes, but for me personally, it was just as much about Michael and all of the kids we met in the Collaborative Classroom back in fifth grade.

My match against Bradley didn't have all of the theatrics that Peter's did, but it was still a great success. For Bradley, though, the best part was receiving his award. He was beaming.

"I'm a champion," he told everyone he saw, showing off the medal he had wrapped around his neck. "I'm a champion."

When the mats were rolled up and the night was over, Terupt found Peter and me. "I've never been prouder of two of my wrestlers," he said.

I never thought I could lose a match and feel like such a winner.

Jessica

After the dust settles . . .
and the last of the matches are wrestled,
the last of the pictures are taken,
the last of the medals are handed out,
and the sounds of the gym
empty
and fade
away,
my teacher decides
it's time for a new
beginning.

He hands me a paper.
It's a flier,

advertising something.
A poetry slam.

I look at him.
"It's your turn, Jessica.
I'm picking your bucket-list event for you."

"What about everyone else?" I ask.
"They need to be involved."

"We'll be there,
rooting from the audience.
It's too perfect an opportunity
to pass up.
You're a natural-born writer."

It's perfect
and scary.
I write poetry
I don't perform it.
I glance at my friends,
my bald friends.

A bald Lexie performing my poem . . .
that could be . . .
epic.

Alexia

We were chillin' in my bedroom when Jess first asked me to perform her poem.

I was like, "Are you serious? I don't know anything about poetry—or slamming it."

But she was like, "Yes, but you know about performing, Lex. You're a star. And I need a star to bring my words to life."

"A star? My hair hasn't even grown back. I'll be the laughingstock of the slam. No way!"

"Lexie, please. Just think about how much fun we'll have getting your outfit ready."

I wanted to tell her she was crazy, but like, how could I? Jess was my best friend. She'd shaved her head with me—for me. And getting all done up did sound fun.

"Fine," I huffed, for dramatic flair.

"Yay!" she cheered, grabbing me in a hug. "Thanks, Lex."

"I still think you're nuts," I said.

"You're going to kill it," she promised, letting go and looking at me.

"*Pfft*. Whatever. Have you written it yet? I need to practice if I'm gonna do this, you know."

And so it began, my journey to becoming a poetry slammer. We spent hours watching videos of professional ones, studying their styles and moves, the way their bodies danced with their words, the way they enunciated, pronunciated, rapped, and rhymed, their voices bringing stories to life. Jessica read poems to me, teaching me about pacing and rhythm and emphasis. She had me reading to her. The more we watched and practiced and rehearsed, the more excited I became. Together, we were gonna kill it.

Together, we transformed into the Poet Jexia.

Jeffrey

This poetry slam thing kinda came out of nowhere. It was a cool idea, and definitely right up Jessica's alley, but it was different from our other bucket-list adventures because we weren't spending lots of time organizing and planning for it. We couldn't even if we'd wanted to. The competition was right around the corner.

But as the slam drew near, it felt increasingly funny not to be doing anything for it when we'd been so involved in all of the other events, so I decided to write my own poem. I'd never written one before, but I didn't want Jessica to feel alone because she was the only one putting her words out there, or Lexie because she was the only one performing. I had their backs. I didn't tell anyone, though. This was my surprise.

* * *

The slam took place at a large restaurant where they had a venue for live performances. It was a cool spot. Once I got a look at the stage and lights, with nothing to hide behind except for a skinny mic stand, I had more nerves than I got before my wrestling matches. I watched a few people go and thankfully they weren't world-class, so I made the decision to get up there and go for it before I changed my mind.

I told the gang I was going to the bathroom, and then I snuck away and found the emcee of the event and told her I had a poem to perform. Simple as that, I was next.

"Please put your hands together for our last-minute newcomer, Jeffrey," she announced when it was my turn.

I took a deep breath and walked out to a smattering of applause.

"No way!" Peter yelled, jumping to his feet.

I gripped the mic stand. "Hi. I'm Jeffrey, but tonight I'm J," I said.

"No way!" Peter yelled again. "Woo-hoo!"

Lexie grabbed his arm and made him sit back down.

I smiled and continued. "This poem is written by me—my first—and will be performed by me—my first. It's called 'Searching.'"

Before Michael left,
a fire lit inside me
that I can't explain.
It burns strong

on the mats,
to be the best,
for him—
because he thought I was.

So I went
without food,
without drink,
without energy,
searching for my best,
but losing much along the way.
Breaking hearts
not including mine
still in pieces.

My coach
and drill partner
picked me up
and put me
on the scale first,
and then on the right path again.

My coach
and drill partner,
always having my back,
on this quest to be the best.

But I went on searching
for a way

to put the pieces
together.
Hers

and mine.

Asher showed us how.
Two hands
becoming one.
Together again,
where I feel strongest
and happiest.
Where I'm
at my best.

Peter

If Jeffrey was doing this poem thing for his girl, then I needed to do one for mine. I didn't have anything planned or written, but once I saw him slamming it I found a pencil and scratched a few words on a napkin. I only got a few lines down before he finished, so I had no choice but to wing it. The joint was still clapping and cheering for him when I climbed onto the stage.

"My name is Dragon Slayer," I said, introducing myself to the audience. That got a few laughs, so I was off to a good start. "My poem is an ode to Lexie."

My boy, Jeffrey,
is not a poet.
This boy (I pointed at my chest)
is not a poet.

But if Jeffrey serenades his girl,
Then I've got to give it a whirl.

"Not a bad start, huh?" I asked the audience after that rhyme. I got a few more laughs, putting me at ease, and then I continued.

Roses are red
Violets are puke
Lexie'd be dead
if not for Luke.

For it wasn't me
or my pee
that saved her.

But Dragon Slayer
is the guy,
who will always try

to have her back
and save her day.
And I'm not talking smack
Jack
Because saving the day.
is just my way.

"I'm Dragon Slayer. Out."
Mic drop.
Boom!

Jessica

Jeffrey surprised everyone when he slipped from his chair and took the stage. He did an incredible job with his poem. Not to be outdone, Peter went next. How should I put this? Let's just say, he was very entertaining.

I was so appreciative that they did that. That they had my back—and Lexie's. Not to sound conceited, but if those two could do it, then Lexie and I knew we could too.

"Please put your hands together for the Poet Jexia," the slam's emcee announced.

There was applause as Lexie took the stage. She strode to the center wearing a sleek black dress. It was one that accentuated her booty—a must. She must've tried on a hundred different scarves before ultimately choosing to go without one, opting instead for her buzzed head. Lastly, she added a touch of power and intimidation to her outfit with a striking violet lipstick. She looked beautiful.

"My name is Alexia. I'm here to perform the words written by my best friend, Jessica. Together, we are the Poet Jexia. This is called 'The One.'"

He's the one
I first met
when he was new to Snow Hill
and I was too.

The one
who changed our classroom
and us
with books
and projects
and class meetings.

The one
who conducted the orchestra,
steered the boat,
and guided our hearts—
even when he was asleep.

He's the one
who has always brought us home,
but has to go now,
and I wish

I had the words
to make it better.
To make it easy.
I don't.

But he's the one
we'll stay together
because of
and for.

The one
we'll miss
and think of
often,
until we see each other
again,
somewhere,
sometime.

Always, he'll be
the one.

When Lexie finished, I walked onto the stage and we
hugged. Then we turned and took a bow together—the Poet
Jexia. Slammed.

The room filled with applause and cheers. Peter was on
his feet again, leading the charge. I noticed Danielle and
Luke had skooched closer to each other, Jeffrey and Anna

were holding hands, and Dad had his arm around Mom—and then my eyes fell on Mr. Terupt.

He held Hope in one arm and was helping his wife out of her chair with his other. Mrs. Terupt had both of her hands on her belly and was taking rapid breaths. There was only one explanation. It was time.

june

Peter

I had good news and bad news. The good news was T got it right and had a son the second time around. A scrappy little wrestler that he and the missus named Thomas. Mrs. T and the baby were happy and healthy and doing great.

What sucked was the gang wasn't gonna get to babysit Thomas. I could've taught him a wrestling stance and read him books about the little train who didn't quit, but that wasn't in the cards. And what sucked even more than that was the bad news. The end was actually here.

My feet dragged on my way to our last advising session. We were actually having a double period of it since it was our last one, so you could say it double sucked. There was no other way to put it. But there was a bright spot hidden in there that I'd forgotten about until Jeffrey reminded me: we had our time capsule from the beginning of the year to open.

Suddenly, I was excited. I couldn't wait for everyone to see what I'd put inside. I picked my feet up and got to T's room as fast as I could. Once we had everyone together, T had us gather around his worktable and then he pulled the capsule down from his top shelf.

"Time for us to open this baby," he said.

I just told you, I couldn't wait—but I had to, because before we got to the opening part, Lukester decided he'd hit us with his surprise bucket-list plans. I was beyond frustrated after we started doing his dumb activity—but it turned out to be exactly what we needed.

LUKE

**IF you have something to look forward to,
THEN that can ease the pain of failure or loss—
or goodbye.**

Let's take Jeffrey or Peter, for example. If Jeffrey were to lose a big match, that would be painful for him, but if he knew there was a chance at a rematch on the horizon, that would help him pick himself up and move forward with even stronger determination. Just ask that Oliver kid—and Jeffrey didn't even lose to him the first time they wrestled.

Now let's consider Danielle. When her grandmother dies, Danielle will undoubtedly feel tremendous loss. It's her faith that will get her through. Her belief that she will one day join her grandmother in heaven.

Why am I sharing this? Because my bucket-list idea was based on this premise. If we had a tomorrow to look forward to with Mr. Terupt, then saying goodbye might be slightly less painful.

"Okay, gang, this is it," Mr. Terupt said after we'd all arrived for our final advising session. He walked over and pulled our time capsule down from the top shelf where it had sat all year. "Time for us to open this baby."

"I can't wait till you see what I stuck in there!" Peter exclaimed.

"Neither can we," Lexie groaned sarcastically.

"Just you wait," Peter snickered. "It's gonna be epic, Lukester."

"Actually, can we do something before you open that?" I asked Mr. Terupt.

"Sure, Luke. What's up?"

"It's time for my bucket-list event," I announced.

"How can it be time for your event when we haven't done anything for it? We don't even know what it is, for crying out loud," Peter griped.

"I've taken care of everything," I assured them.

My friends began exchanging glances to see who knew what, but they were all just as lost as Peter. I hadn't shared my idea with anyone. Once they realized this, Jessica turned and asked, "What do you have planned?"

I reached into my bag and pulled out a deck of cards and a pair of dice.

"Gambling!" Peter cheered. "What're we playing, strip poker?"

"You wish!" Lexie cried, slugging Peter in the shoulder.

Mr. Terupt shook his head, which was about all you could do with those two. I pulled out my notebook and a pencil next. Then I found a blank page and drew a quick chart with each of our names listed down the side and *Round 1*, *Round 2*, and *Round 3* written across the top.

"Okay. Everyone needs to take a turn rolling the dice. I will record your results under Round 1," I directed.

There were plenty of puzzled looks, but they went along with it. Jeffrey picked up the dice, gave them a shake, and let them roll. "Seven," he said.

"The most likely outcome," I mumbled. "Hopefully we don't get too many of those."

Anna went next. "Ten."

Danielle followed. "Three."

We continued taking turns, Mr. Terupt included. He had to participate in order for it to qualify as a true bucket-list event.

Peter was the last to go before me. "Twelve!" he yelled. "That's the highest. What do I win?"

"Nothing yet," I said.

"Grrr," he growled, clearly not happy with my answer. He shoved the dice across the table.

I gave them a shake and rolled. Eleven. I recorded my number. Then I put the dice on the side and picked up the cards and began shuffling.

"For the second round, you need to pull three cards from the deck," I explained. "You can do anything you want with your three cards—"

"Stick them up your butt," Peter interrupted.

"Up *your* butt," Lexie retaliated.

Mr. Terupt scowled.

"Sorry. I had to say it," Peter said, and shrugged.

"As I was explaining," I continued, "you can do any mathematical operation with your three cards, but your resulting number must be a value between one and thirty-one."

We took our turns and came up with a range of numbers. I recorded the results.

"This is your bucket-list event?" Peter complained, unable to hide his disappointment any longer. To be honest, I was surprised he'd lasted this long. "I had higher hopes for you, Lukester. We could be bungee jumping or zip lining. Instead you've got us playing some wacko game with rules that make zero sense. No offense, but this is stupid."

"Peter, you know better," Mr. Terupt scolded. "No project idea of Luke's has ever been stupid. Let him finish."

Did Mr. Terupt see what I was doing, or just trust me? I wondered. He looked at me and nodded.

"The final round is your choice," I continued. "You can roll four times or pull four cards, or do some combination of the two, but you need four numbers in the end, and you must use the four numbers same as you did in the last round, but this time we want an end value between twenty-one and ninety-nine."

Once again, Jeffrey went first. Anna followed and then Danielle after her. It was uneventful until Peter got his turn and, miraculously, he pulled all four aces from the deck.

"Wow!" he freaked. "Good thing we're not playing strip poker. You'd all be na-ked!"

"You couldn't do that again in a million years," Jeffrey said.

"No kidding! And I don't even win anything!" Peter whined.

I chose to ignore him and took my turn, opting to roll twice and pull two cards. I recorded my number. And that was it. The chart was complete. I tore a clean page from my notebook and began listing our results.

JEFFREY: 7-27

ANNA: 10-6

DANIELLE: 3-10

JESSICA: 8-31

LEXIE: 6-25

MR. TERUPT: 9-12

LUKE: 11-13

PETER: 12-25

"They're dates," Peter said, when he saw what I was doing.

"No duh. Thanks, Captain Obvious," Jeffrey jeered.

"Shut up," Peter growled.

While they bickered, I finished by adding the resulting year to each of the dates listed.

"The question is, what do these dates signify?" Jessica asked.

"That is the question," I agreed. "First off, these dates are nonnegotiable. They are to be etched in stone. Is that clear?"

"Why?" Peter asked.

"Etched in stone," I repeated forcefully. "Got it?"

"Okay, okay," Peter said, holding up his hands. "But why? What's the big deal about these dates?"

"Everyone understands the conditions?" I asked the group. "The dates are nonnegotiable."

They nodded.

"Good. Then here's the big deal: on each of these dates, we promise to reconvene—all seven of us and Mr. Terupt. No excuses and no questions asked."

It took a minute for what I'd just said to register, but then I saw them analyzing our list and thinking about what things might look like for us on these different occasions.

"We're going to spend a Christmas together?" Anna asked, referring to Peter's date.

"Yes!" Peter roared. "You heard Lukester. This is nonnegotiable."

I smiled.

"We'll be old fogies when we get together on this one," Jeffrey pointed out.

"Yup," I agreed.

"Will Teach even be—" Lexie started, and then came up short.

"Maybe," Mr. Terupt said. "Maybe not. But I like the thought of all of you getting together even after I'm gone, if that's the case."

"Thanks, Luke," Danielle said.

"Yes, thank you," Jessica echoed.

"You knew what you were doing when you thought of this one, Lukester," Peter said. "It's impossible for me to tell you how much it means."

Lexie reached up and cupped Peter's face, planting a kiss square on his lips. "You are the sweetest," she said.

Peter's face turned fifty shades of red.

Then Lexie turned to me. "I could kiss you too, but I'll leave that to Danielle."

My face and Danielle's turned the other fifty shades of red.

"One thing's for sure," Mr. Terupt said, "we can definitely look forward to getting together again. It's not goodbye. It's see you later."

Peter

"All right. Enough with the mushiness," I said, bringing an end to Luke's bucket-list game. A guy can only handle so much of that sentimental stuff. "Let's open the capsule."

"Peter's right," T agreed. It wasn't often that I heard that. "We better get to it before we run out of time."

"How should we proceed?" Jessica asked.

"What do you mean? Tip it over and dump everything out," I said.

"No!" Lexie objected. "There's no fun in that. It needs to be slower and way more dramatic."

"Ugh," I moaned.

"How about I reach in and pull one item out at a time?" T suggested.

"That's better," Lexie agreed. "Let's do that."

Everyone nodded in agreement. I didn't care. I just wanted to get started.

T opened the top and pulled out the first item. It was a Magic 8 Ball. Jeffrey was the culprit. It was one of those key-chain ones, but it still did the trick.

We passed it around and immediately started reminiscing about the events of our party in seventh grade when we got together to wait for the results of the budget vote. It was funny telling T how I got Lexie with the whipped-cream prank. She didn't think it was too funny, but that just made it even funnier. I had a few killer questions that I could've asked the 8-ball right then that would've had everyone in an uproar, but I decided to keep them to myself so that we could move on to the next item in the capsule.

It went like that for a while, until there was only one item left. "Save the best for last," I crowed.

T reached in and pulled out my item.

"What the heck?" Jeffrey said.

"You're disgusting!" Lexie shrieked.

T shook his head and Danielle covered her eyes.

"It's a copy of the butt prank! Remember how awesome that was?" I shouted.

"Not very," a voice from the doorway responded.

We looked up. It was Principal Lee. Timing is everything.

"I came by to see if I could snap a picture of the gang," he said. "I knew I'd find you together during advising, but I wasn't expecting this." He pointed at the butt.

"You want a picture of us?" I asked. "Why?"

"Because you're the reason I'm bald!" he exclaimed. "And because . . . just because."

"Don't worry, Principal Lee," Lexie said. "We get it."

For once, I agreed with her.

We stood together in back of T's classroom, posing for Mr. Lee, and right before he snapped his pic I stuck the butt next to Lexie's head and smiled wide.

"Ugh," Lexie huffed, yanking the photocopy out of my hands. She wadded it up and tossed it into the trash.

"Thank you, Miss Johnson," Lee said. "Now let's try it again."

"The first one was perfect," I protested.

Lexie stomped on my foot and Lee snapped his next pic at the exact moment I was yelling in pain.

Timing is everything.

Thanks to Lukester, we had a bunch of dates to look forward to, and thanks to Principal Lee, we had a picture capturing one of our final days together to remember until the next time. Principal Lee was cool and gave each of us a framed copy on the last day of school. What was even cooler was I got the one with the butt in it.

"Good luck, Mr. Jacobs. And if you need anything next year, you come and find me," Principal Lee said.

"Thanks."

We shook hands and I walked out of the junior high with my picture and all my memories, ready for high school and the next phase of my life—but summer first. A guy needs his summer vacation.

Alexia

Mom and I were waiting for Vincent to get home from the restaurant so we could go to Danielle's for the big Goodbye Teach Family celebration. I was standing in front of the bathroom mirror, modeling different head scarves to see which one went best with my outfit. This was a special occasion, so like, I needed to look good. I was tying a deep-green one behind my head when Mom came in.

"Remember when you helped me with these things?" she said, taking the fabric from my hands and knotting it for me.

I looked at her reflection in the mirror and smiled.

"You look beautiful," she whispered.

"Thanks, Mom."

And like, the next thing I knew she'd spun me around and had me in a firm hug.

"Mom! Like, what the heck?" I gasped. "Are you all right?"

"I opened your results," she blurted, hiding her face against my neck. "I wasn't snooping, I swear. I found the envelope when I was putting away your laundry."

I couldn't breathe.

"You don't have the cancer gene." She choked, and leaned back and looked me in the eye. A mix of tears and mascara ran down her cheeks. She pulled the paper from her pocket and showed me.

The crushing weight that had been on my chest a second ago lifted. I breathed. "No cancer," I whispered.

Mom shook her head. "I'm sorry I opened it, Lexie. I told you we could wait. But when I came across it—"

"It's okay," I said. "I wanted you to find it."

Margo yipped from the bathroom, where she sat on the toilet lid, watching us.

"No cancer, Margo," I told her, and smiled.

"You'll still need to be vigilant and get regular checkups when you're older," Mom insisted, wiping her face. "These tests are no guarantees, and they only look at a few select variants of the gene."

"I know and I will," I promised.

We hugged again, and then I caught sight of my reflection in the mirror. Mom wasn't the only one with mascara streaks running down her cheeks.

"We've got to get cleaned up!" I exclaimed. "We can't go to a party looking like this!"

Margo barked in agreement, her little tail pattering against the potty. Mom and I looked at her and started laughing.

"Whoa!" Vincent shouted, surprising us. He'd picked the perfect moment to show up. "Didn't realize I was picking up KISS," he said.

"Funny," Mom replied.

"Gross!" I yelled, slugging him in the arm.

"Ow," he whined, playing along.

"No cancer gene," Mom said, showing him my results.

Vincent pulled Mom and me into a hug, which got the two of us crying again. "That's wonderful news," he said, kissing the top of my head.

Margo barked again and I giggled. This was going to be one of my best and hardest days mixed together. No cancer gene, but I still needed to stop at CVS on my way to Danielle's so I could pay for the GeneLink kit that I stole months ago. Mom wasn't about to let that go. And like, then I had to find the strength to do the really hard stuff. I had to say goodbye to Mr. and Mrs. Teach, my little fashionista Hope, and baby Thomas.

Danielle

Grandma made everyone come to our house on the day we had to say goodbye. She insisted that we gather around the table—tables, in this case, because there were so many of us—to share a meal and prayer before . . . you know. All I could think was that we were having our very own Last Supper.

Grandma and Mom had spent the past two days preparing the feast. They baked a slew of pies and had too many side dishes. Vincent contributed a ziti platter with these incredible meatballs and a beautiful lemon-based chicken from his restaurant. Poor Peter's mouth was watering by the time we had everyone together and took seats around the glorious spread. It smelled delicious.

"Mrs. Roberts, would you mind if I led the prayer?" Mr. Terupt asked Grandma before we passed any food.

"Please," Grandma said. "I think that would be nice."

We joined hands and bowed our heads. Mr. Terupt began, "Dear Lord,

We thank you for this amazing food, the gorgeous weather, and the opportunity to be together. But mostly, we thank you for the past four years. We've grown and learned and become better people because of each other. We ask that you be with us as we continue our journeys ahead— until our paths bring us together again. Amen."

On cue, my pump began playing Beethoven, which was perfect because none of us knew how to break the silence after Mr. Terupt's heartfelt words. Everyone laughed about the sudden music and then started chatting and fixing plates and passing dishes around the table. I tended to my pump and then joined in.

The food not only *smelled* delicious, it *was* delicious. Having everyone together was the best part, though. It was a gathering as special as any holiday, but it had to come to an end. After dessert and more storytelling and talk, Mr. Terupt took a breath and pushed back from the table, signaling this was it. He stood and stretched and the room immediately fell silent. He picked up his plate and his wife's. "Mrs. Roberts, where can I take these for you?" he asked Grandma.

"Nowhere," Grandma replied. "Just leave them right there. Debbie and I will take care of it. You go on outside with your family and the kids and get on your way."

"You're sure?" Mr. Terupt asked.

"Yes."

"Thank you for the wonderful meal," Mr. Terupt said.

"Can't send you away on an empty stomach," Grandma said. She walked around to his side of the table and gave my teacher a hard hug. "You be good," she croaked. Then she grabbed Mr. Terupt's plates and hurried off into the kitchen. Even she needed to make her goodbye quick. That was the farmer's way. Keep busy.

The rest of the women did the same as Grandma. A thank-you and quick hug and then to the kitchen. The men shook hands. Asher did a bit of both. He shook hands with Mr. Terupt but hugged Hope.

"Oh, how sweet," Lexie cooed.

"Do you think those two could have a long-distance relationship?" Anna whispered. "They make a cute couple."

I shook my head and giggled at her matchmaking. The gang and I got up then and went outside. Dragging out the inevitable was not the answer. We'd stretched it as far as we could. It was best to make everything from this point forth as painless as possible.

I steeled myself for what was next. There would be silent hugs with Mr. and Mrs. Terupt and Hope—hugs that said all that we couldn't speak without falling to pieces—and gentle touches and blown kisses for the baby. And then we'd stand together and watch one of the best families any of us had ever known drive off into the distance.

Was I ready?

I'd never be ready, but it was time.

Jessica

Mr. Terupt handed . . .
a set of keys
to my father.
"All yours," he said.
"Thanks," Dad replied.

Confused,
I turned to my father.
"What are those for?" I asked.
"To our new house," he answered.

"Wait. Did you buy Mr. Terupt's house?" I asked,
still confused.
"Yes," Mom replied. "It's the perfect size
for a family of three."

I looked
back
                                    and forth
        between
the two of them.

"I'm ready to try," Mom said,
taking my father's hand.
I hugged them both.

Mr. Terupt handed
me
my family.

Jeffrey

After Terupt's car disappeared we were left shell-shocked, like a team that had just suffered a stunning defeat. We were numb with disbelief. Frozen, without a clue of what to do next.

It wasn't Danielle's pump breaking the silence this time. Who was always there, ready to pick me up at times like this? You guessed it.

"See cows!" Asher yelled from behind us, breaking our trances.

We turned around and saw my little toddler brother running toward us. "See cows!" he yelled again. "Ree! See cows!"

"Sorry," Mom called from the doorway. "I kept him in here as long as I could."

"It's okay, Mrs. Mahar," Anna said. "We'll take him."

"Thank you, Anna," Mom replied.

Asher grabbed my hand and Anna's and started pulling us in the direction of the calf pen. He wasn't waiting. He remembered where they were, and we were going. "See cows," he announced all happy.

"See you guys later," I told the others. "Guess we're going to see the cows."

They laughed.

"Bye, Asher," Danielle called, but my little brother was too busy humming and singing to himself to hear her. He never slowed down.

The calves were grown now, so the pen was empty. But Anna brought us to a nearby pasture. Asher released our hands and leaned against the fence when we got there. "Moo!" he yelled to the cows on the other side.

Two cows stood not that far from us, and both stopped and looked in our direction, ears twitching in the breeze.

"They see you, Asher," Anna whispered.

His eyes grew wide. Then he stuck his arm through the rails, trying to touch one.

Anna whistled, and almost instantly the tan-colored cow started ambling in our direction. "She's coming to say hello," Anna whispered to Asher.

He giggled.

"Her name is Bessie," Anna said. "She's my favorite."

"Bussie," Asher repeated. "Favit."

Anna glanced at me and smiled. I watched Bessie walk

up to my little brother, sniff his hand, and give his fingers a big slobbery lick.

Asher squealed. "Kissed me!" he yelled. "Cow kissed me!"

"She sure did, buddy," I said, and laughed.

He pulled his arm back through the fence and turned around. "You kiss," he said, pointing at Anna and me. "You kiss," he repeated, giggling and clapping.

I didn't want my little brother to get upset. What choice did I have?

ANNA

"Kiss!" Asher cheered, clapping and bouncing up and down.

Jeffrey looked at me. "He might get mad if we don't follow his orders."

"We wouldn't want that," I whispered.

"No, we wouldn't," Jeffrey said, stepping closer and leaning in.

I closed my eyes and felt Jeffrey's lips press against mine. It was everything I'd imagined—except for Asher squealing on the sideline. But if it weren't for him, we might still be broken instead of stronger than ever. I wasn't the only matchmaker in town.

That little boy made one of the saddest days of my life one of my happiest.

Peter

It didn't matter how much I tried telling myself I was ready. I wasn't. And time wasn't the answer. I'd never be ready to watch one of the most important people in my life drive away.

But he did. And I just stood there, staring into the distance even after he'd disappeared from sight, because I didn't know what else to do. Luckily, after Lexie hugged Jessica goodbye, she came and took my hand.

"Let's go for a walk," she said.

It was her turn to take care of me. T was gone, but we were still looking out for each other. That wasn't going to stop just because he wasn't around. We were going to be okay. Why? Because our time with T had bound us together forever—in ways nothing else could. It was that special—and I was lucky to have experienced it.

LUKE

IF Mr. Terupt moves away with his family,
THEN it will be hard for the gang, but by sticking
together we will continue to make him proud from afar.

Making Mr. Terupt proud was a lifelong project, and I only
got the best grades on my projects, so this was a no-brainer.
It was the other proof that had me stumped.

IF the gang leaves only Danielle and me standing
together after Mr. Terupt departs,
THEN am I supposed to make some sort of move?

THEN what happens?

Jessica

Goodbye, Mr. Terupt . . .
I whisper,
staring at his taillights,
fading in the distance.
My eyes tear,
but my mouth smiles;
my heart hurts,
but it is full.

Goodbye, Mr. Terupt,
I whisper
standing in his old house,
my new house,
Hope's old bedroom,

now my bedroom—in need of a drastic Lexie
  makeover.

Goodbye, Mr. Terupt,
I whisper.
Till we meet again,
thank you.
Thank you so much,
for everything.

EPILOGUE

Mr. Terupt

"Hey, hon. Come look at this," Sara called from the other room.

"C'mon, Hope. Let's go see what Mommy wants." I scooped up my daughter and carried her into the kitchen, where Sara was busy unpacking yet another box.

"What's up?" I asked.

"I found this."

Sara handed me a beautiful drawing of the gang. Each kid in the sketch held a letter above his or her head spelling out the word *WELCOME*. And below the kids was a sketch of Hope. She was sitting on top of the word *HOME*.

"Danielle must've drawn this for us," I said.

"How sweet of her. Do you think each of the kids hid something?"

I looked at her. "Oh, no."

"What?"

"If they did, that means Peter has a surprise waiting for us inside one of these boxes."

"Oh, no," Sara replied.

"Uh-oh," Hope chirped.

"Exactly. Uh-oh," I agreed. "Keep going," I told Sara, "but be careful. And let me know if you come across anything that seems suspicious."

"Uh-oh," Hope chirped again.

I returned to my box in the living room, and Hope stayed in the kitchen helping Sara. By the end of the day, we'd done some serious unpacking and had discovered a beautiful poem from Jessica, a multiple-choice test from Luke where all of the answers were "The Gang," a fashion scarf that was for Hope or Sara left by Lexie, a rectangular block of wood with Hope's name cut out of it that Jeffrey must've created with my jigsaw, and a thumb drive loaded with photographs of the gang. My favorite was the shot of them huddled around Hope on her play mat. It was clear all of the kids were involved in this surprise project. I could hear Luke's excitement now. But still missing was whatever Peter had stashed away.

I had just finished reading a bedtime story to Hope and was on my last box for the night when I came across another something. "I think I've got it!" I yelled to Sara.

She came into the room carrying Thomas and I showed her the tiny gift-wrapped box. "From Peter?" she said. "All wrapped up?"

"It's wrapped, but not perfectly," I pointed out. "This has tricky Peter written all over it."

"Be careful," Sara warned.

I peeled the paper away and slowly lifted the lid of the box. Nothing jumped out, so I peeked inside. There was a scrap of paper. I pulled it out and read it aloud.

Hey T,

Did you smell it? I left you a fart in the box. Now your new place will smell like home sweet home.

Your favorite,
Peter

"Are you sure you're going to miss him?" Sara asked.

"I already do."

ACKNOWLEDGMENTS

I'd first like to acknowledge my Mr. Terupt fans. Your continued enthusiasm gave me the inspiration and courage to write this book. Thank you.

A big thank-you to the North Andover wrestling team for welcoming me into their practice room, giving me great workouts, and helping me recharge mentally. Wrestle'Lympics is an annual event held in this special community, and after learning about it, I was excited to find a place for it in this story. Amazing work!

I owe tremendous thanks to Beverly Horowitz for her guidance, support, and friendship. The same goes for my agent, Paul Fedorko.

Thank you to Chelan Ecija and Jinna Shin, artist and designer, respectively, for the beautiful new covers for the whole series. I love them!

My eternal gratitude to Françoise Bui. I can't express how happy it makes me that I was able to finish my Mr. Terupt series with you as my editor—the same person who helped me get it started those many years ago. I'm beyond grateful for the opportunity to work with you. Thank you!

Lastly, my family. Thank you to Lily and Anya for cheering me on to the finish line—and for getting me away from the computer and into the pool! And to Beth and Emma. You can add in-home editor to your titles. As always, your feedback on my early drafts was incredibly helpful and—I hesitate to say this—smart. I won't say who helps most. Love you all!

ABOUT THE AUTHOR

ROB BUYEA taught third and fourth graders for six years; then he taught high school biology and coached wrestling for seven years. Currently, he is a full-time writer and lives in Massachusetts with his wife and daughters. He is the author of the Perfect Score series. His first novel, *Because of Mr. Terupt*, was selected as an E. B. White Read Aloud Honor Book and a Cybils Honor Book. It has also won seven state awards and was named to numerous state reading lists. *Goodbye Mr. Terupt; Mr. Terupt Falls Again*; and *Saving Mr. Terupt* are companion novels to *Because of Mr. Terupt*.

robbuyea.com

Seven kids.
Seven voices.
One special teacher
who brings them together.

DON'T MISS **ROB BUYEA's**

MR. TERUPT SERIES

Delacorte
Press

FROM
ROB BUYEA
THE AUTHOR OF THE BELOVED
MR.TERUPT series

There's more to middle school than getting the perfect score

Delacorte Press